THE HOUSE ON THE CROSSROADS

A novella by

Julia Guthrie

Copyright © 2025 Julia Guthrie

All rights reserved

The characters and events portrayed in this book are fictitious. Any similarity to real persons, living or dead, is coincidental and not intended by the author.

No part of this book may be reproduced, or stored in a retrieval system, or transmitted in any form or by any means, electronic, mechanical, photocopying, recording, or otherwise, without express written permission of the publisher.
Cover design by:J. Guthrie

*Thank you to my Husband for all of your support
and encouragement over the years.
Thank you also, to my parents and dear friends
for your wonderful feedback. It is, as always,
invaluable to me.
The locations in this book are both a
mixture of real and invented, however they
are based on real places in West Cornwall
where I lived for almost 20 years.*

CONTENTS

Title Page
Copyright
Dedication
Chapter 1 - Penmerryn Cove   1
Chapter 2 - Whispers of the past   8
Chapter 3 - Four lanes   18
Chapter 4 - The magnolia tree   24
Chapter 5 - Darkness falls   30
Chapter 6 - Mr Blackthorn   37
Chapter 7 - Things that are hidden   50
Chapter 8 - Ellie   69
Chapter 9 - Carn Madrow   83
Chapter 10 - Tom   97
Chapter 11 - The Order Of Decay   107
Chapter 12 - Wintertide   117
Chapter 13 - Bound by chaos   129
Chapter 14 - Secrets   140
Chapter 15 - The house on the crossroads   154
Chapter 16 - Darkest before the dawn   170

Chapter 17 - A debt must always be paid   180

CHAPTER 1 - PENMERRYN COVE

Daniel squinted into the gloomy half light as the windscreen wipers clunked lazily back and forth. They provided only brief glimpses of clarity before the incessant Cornish drizzle blurred their view again. Grace sighed despairingly from the passenger seat as yet another unhelpful road sign loomed. It had taken them over six hours to get here, and two of those had been spent navigating the dreaded London traffic.

A single track road wound through an almost alien landscape of stubby, windswept trees and shrubs sprouting from low, roughly stacked granite walls known as 'Cornish hedges'. Surrounding the car on both sides, they didn't make driving any easier, especially in this weather, when visibility was next to zero and passing places were few and far between. Meanwhile the sat nav helpfully barked instructions that bore scant resemblance to the road they currently travelled.

Bare left and then take the next right...

"Bare left?" Scowled Daniel. "There's one

road and we're on it."

"If you can call it a road." Grace muttered. Equally as fed up with the long journey, now approaching the seven hour mark.

The sat nav had now seemingly given up, wisely determining it safer to stay silent as they approached a crossroads. Daniel slowed the car to a halt.

"Now which way?" He grumbled. "Where the hell are we? I haven't even seen the sea yet."

Grace fumbled for her phone to check google maps again. "Still no internet - it's useless!"

"I'll just go straight over. Keep an eye out for any road signs, Penmerryn must be on one of them."

"Hang on, there's a bloke over there walking a dog - I'll ask…" She wound down the window and called out, "Hello? Do you know where Penmerryn Cove is?"

The man and his dog - a liver and white springer spaniel, paused in unison, ears pricked, before moving toward the car. The middle aged man was swathed in a big woollen coat, scarf, hat, and somewhat scraggly beard. "Aye, I do indeed. You're in it." He drawled, "You's down for a Winter holiday?"

He rested a hand on the car door as an excited springer leapt up to demand a pat on the head from the occupants to which Grace happily obliged. "Ah, no. Umm, we're actually looking for a place called Fourlanes House."

The man fiddled with his hat. "Well now - You mean ol' John Padget's place?"

Daniel leaned over, suddenly more intrigued."Yes. He was my Uncle. You knew him?"

"Aye, I knew John. Good fella he was. Such a shame to lose him. Your Uncle you say?"

"Yes. Sadly I'd not seen him for many years. We've never been close. We've inherited the house - it's as all a bit of a surprise to tell the truth. Oh, I'm Daniel, and this is my wife, Grace."

"Terry Trenoweth, pleased to meet you."

They shook hands. The dog gave a loud bark. Terry chuckled. "And this ere's Bramble. Guess we'll be neighbours then." He waved an arm towards the lane he'd appeared from. "We're at the old farm cottage, end of the lane. Where you from then?"

"London." Replied Grace.

"Oh that's a fair old way."

"You're not wrong. And these roads take some getting used to."

Terry gave a raspy chuckle. "Aye. They do indeed. Anyway, you'll be wanting to get home so I won't keep you. Just turn right, and then it's a sharp left to Fourlanes, the driveway's easy to miss. Drop by once you're settled, the missus will be pleased to meet you." He gave a nod, and a whistle to the dog who was already bored with the interruption and now scrabbling in the bushes after some small creature.

They parted company with a wave. The turning was obscured by trees and they did indeed almost miss it. Daniel swung the car onto the gravel driveway with a crunch and they sat in silence for a moment, taking it all in. The house was much larger than they'd imagined it would be. Imposing mottled Victorian granite stone blocks rose to meet the ever darkening grey sky above.

A scrubby patch of garden spilled over onto the driveway, vanishing around the back of the house; further lined with trees and brambles.

Grace cast a wary eye as they eased themselves out of their seats. "Looks like it could use a bit of TLC. Your Uncle wasn't much of a gardener was he?"

Daniel grimaced.

Turning back towards the car, Grace gasped in annoyance. "Bloody hell, the poor chap's not been dead five minutes and some idiots have been up here messing about already!"

"What's up?" Daniel followed her gaze and spotted the graffiti covering the modest stone pillars that marked the entrance. "What is that nonsense?" He marched over for a closer look at the curious swirls and strange lettering in black paint. "A pentagram - is that even still a thing? Kids today believe in that black magic rubbish.?"

"I doubt it. They probably just think it's funny. We'll scrub it off tomorrow, right now I just need a cup of tea and a shower. God - I hope there's hot water!"

"You open up, I'll grab some bags."

With that, the rain began in earnest. Murky drizzle to downpour in seconds. Grace pulled up the hood on her jacket as she struggled to get the key into the lock. She yelled back to Daniel, "Are you sure this is the right key? It won't fit!"

Daniel appeared by her side, dropping the bags onto the wet paving. "I hope so!" He watched her make two more futile attempts then held out his hand. "Give it here." The key slotted into the lock on the first try. They blinked at each other. "Maybe it was just stiff." He shrugged.

They fell into the house in a puddle of water, scattering wet luggage and stripping off their coats. The silence yawned eerily around them. A wooden rail wound up two flights of stairs while a hallway stretched out before them, lined with doors. Even with furniture still in place it had all the ambience of an abandoned house. Grace shivered. "Need to get the heating on. Feels like a tomb in here."

Daniel peered into a couple of rooms, switching on lights as he went, and called out. "Kitchen's in here...So's the boiler by the looks of it."

Grace followed the sound of his voice. "Wow! Not at all what I was expecting. Bit scruffy but very 'farmhouse kitchen'. It's even got a fireplace!"

She unpacked the small travel bag, getting

to work on the refreshments, meanwhile Daniel had found what he was looking for and the central heating clicked into gear, radiators popped and crackled into life and the smell of burning dust permeated the damp air.

They huddled for a moment with their steaming mugs of tea and stared about them, feeling a little lost, and extremely tired. Eventually plucking up the courage to explore, they wandered from room to room, cautiously peering round doors as though they might be intruding on someone living there, not quite realising that they were now the occupants. The rooms were cosy. They found more fireplaces and vowed to get them cleaned out and working as soon as possible. As they reached the master bedroom on the top floor, Grace was drawn to the huge bay window. "Look, I think you can actually see the sea!" She smiled into the falling darkness. "Can you believe it? Last time I went to the seaside was a day trip to Hastings with my Grandparents, and as I recall the tide was well and truly out."

Daniel chuckled, "Are you finally excited now?"

She pulled a face and stuck out her tongue.

Daniel sidled up to his wife, putting his arms around her waist. "I want us to be happy here. I know this is all a bit sudden, but getting this opportunity just feels like a good omen."

"If you ignore all the hassle we had trying to find the place." Grace joked.

"Well, yeah… ignore that bit obviously."

The clouds suddenly parted to reveal a low, heavy moon on the horizon. A glittering path of silver cut through the darkness and lay shimmering atop the distant waves. Daniel sighed happily. "It's gonna be good here Grace. Things will be so much better for us here, I promise."

"I know." She answered gently. "And it'll be our first Christmas in Cornwall!"

"What d'ya think they do down here? Christmas dinner on the beach?" He chuckled.

"Well if not, I don't see why we can't start a new tradition!" She laughed at him. Smiling to herself at all the brand new possibilities laid out before them. Things would be different here and she was determined to make it so.

CHAPTER 2 - WHISPERS OF THE PAST

The thriving village of Penmerryn was only minutes down the hill, with a few small shops, pub and a bakery / tea room all facing onto a pretty harbourside. Probably more for the tourists' benefit these days, than the families who owned the few tiny fishing boats pulled up on the golden sand, but it seemed busy enough even at this time of year.

The nearest town was another twenty minute drive away, and after battling her way round a somewhat smaller supermarket than she was used to, Grace heaved the bags of food and cleaning supplies into the boot of the car and slammed it shut. A cold wind stung her cheeks, but she stood for a moment soaking up the glorious November sunshine. Today was officially the first day of the rest of their lives.

She'd only been to Cornwall once before, when she was a teenager. A typical camping holiday with the parents. Busy campsite, over priced gift shop, over crowded beach complete with wall to wall towels and windbreakers. It hadn't been all that much fun, but this felt different. Cornwall in the Winter was always more subdued, but here, in the very depths of the West Country, things seemed permanently sleepy, and much less touristy. Grace basked in the peace and quiet of it all, as she drove the narrow roads past rows of granite cottages, and sweeping stretches of moorland topped with the most stunning blue seascape she'd ever seen. Everything seemed so small compared to London, and yet at the same time so vast. She wound down the window to let the fresh sea air blast her face and tangle her chestnut curls, as she sang along to some random song on the radio. She couldn't remember when she'd last felt so happy. She passed locals walking their dogs along the winding cliff path, hair and clothes alike blown into all manner of craziness by that ever prevalent Cornish wind. Dogs barked and ran happily in circles, toddlers pointed and giggled from their pushchairs. It was a perfect Tuesday morning. She made a mental note of where the path began so they could return and do that walk themselves very soon.

Slowing to allow the car ahead to pull in next to a school, she saw children milling about in the playground chattering excitedly while their teachers attempted to keep order. They appeared to be preparing for some kind of festival. Some of them held aloft hand painted lanterns on sticks, whilst others sported curious looking masks and headdresses with antlers and greenery entwined evocatively around them. A hand made, laminated sign was tied to the gate - *Penmerryn Wintertide - Festival Of Lights - 21st December, 7pm* - Another mental note was added.

Pulling into the driveway back at Fourlanes House, she spied a familiar white van and jumped out just as Holly & Adam appeared from within the house, Daniel in tow, to fetch another box.

"GRACE!!" Holly rushed to embrace her with a massive bear hug. "What a place! It's incredible."

"It's not too bad…" Grace smiled sheepishly. "Thank you so much for bringing our stuff down. You guys are the best!"

Adam stooped and gave her a quick, manly hug before scooping up some more boxes and heading back indoors, calling over his shoulder "Don't worry, we'll be holidaying here from now on… you can repay us in Pasties."

Holly laughed, "You do that, you'll never get rid of him, but seriously… this is a dream come true! Here, let me give you a hand with all that.

The girls unloaded the shopping, then joined Daniel & Adam for a proper tour of the house. They'd been friends for over ten years and had many adventures together up in the 'big smoke'. Adam owned a handyman business and had offered the use of his van to transport their belongings, not that there was much to bring.

Their tiny flat in Croydon had barely needed any furnishings. A few sentimental pieces passed down from family, and a suitcase each of clothes. "We travel light!" Daniel had quipped.

Two hours later the sun still shone. Four coffees and four large Cornish pasties were eagerly purchased from the local bakery on the quay, and four happy, twenty-somethings lounged on the damp sand, throwing pebbles into the waves and munching rich, salty pastry filled with - melt in your mouth - beef and potato without a care in the world.

Holly dragged Grace for a paddle in the icy water, watched by a few bemused locals with raised eyebrows. Adam moved to a rock closer to his friend and sipped his coffee. "So what's the verdict mate? Good decision?"

Daniel watched his Wife splashing and laughing in the water and smiled. "Yeh. Definitely."

"You don't think you'll be lonely down here? We don't want you getting bored." Adam snickered.

"Bored my ass... you've seen that house! I'm gonna be re-decorating for the rest of my life!"

"Nah. Family mate. It's a long way. Your Mum's not getting any younger, I know you've not always seen eye to eye, but with all that's happened?"

"I know what you're saying, but it feels right.

Grace & I need some time on our own. This is a good opportunity. Mum's ok with it, and I think getting out of London is what I need too."

"Fair enough, but make sure you keep in touch. Don't shut us out. Anything you need, just ask, OK? Anything!"

Daniel nodded. "We'll be OK, I can feel it. This is meant to be."

Adam eyed him uneasily. "Fair enough mate. You'd best convert one of those bedrooms into a holiday apartment though, cuz Holly's gonna be nagging at me to get back down in the summer."

Daniel laughed. "Yeh, but it'll cost ya…."

"Tight bastard!" Adam roared. "After all the favours we've done you!"

As if on cue, Holly yelled from the water's edge, "Oy, are you two coming for a paddle? Or does a bit of cold water scare you?"

"Are you mad?" Adam snorted. "I can't drive home with frostbite."

"Challenge accepted!" Whooped Daniel. "Come on you wuss" He punched Adam playfully in the shoulder as they raced each other to the water's edge, hopping in and out of the waves with shouts of surprise. Serious conversations long forgotten. The remainder of their day was spent meandering around the village. A supermarket pizza and lagers all round in front of a bad horror movie ended the couple's visit as they were up early for the long and tedious drive back to London.

Daniel and Grace waved them off in their pyjamas from the front door.

"I'm gonna miss them."

"Yeah..." Murmured Daniel. "But I don't miss London, do you?"

She shook her head.

"What's in that bag over there?" Daniel inquired.

"Some housewarming gifts; cake and some bottles of wine. They know us too well." Grace grinned.

Daniel dived on it, holding aloft the family pack of Tunnocks tea cakes with a triumphant shout.

Grace laughed, rescuing the treats and stashing them back into the bag. "Leave those, we've got work to do before lunch. There's a house to clean, remember?"

"Slave driver."

"It's the reason you love me!" She laughed, throwing him a pack of cleaning cloths.

The house itself wasn't in too bad shape, but they had deemed it in need of a good clean, new curtains and some air fresheners. The bathroom and kitchen fittings were surprisingly modern and it seemed like Uncle John had done a fair bit of DIY in recent years, for which they were grateful.

Grace immediately flung open all the windows and once everything had been scrubbed to within an inch of its life, and the brand new bedding in place, she paused to admire their efforts. The redecorating would take a bit of time mind you, paint and wallpaper sure wasn't cheap, but it was perfectly livable for the time being. It made a nice change to be thinking like this. Ordinary life decisions. Normal and satisfyingly dull. She left Daniel sorting through the massive antique wardrobe in the spare room, seemingly full of junk, to fetch a celebratory glass of wine. Only to discover that her sneaky friends had left a bottle of Champagne in the fridge. She poured two glasses and giggled to herself, envisioning the look of surprise on her Husband's face when she returned.

Creeping carefully back up the stairs she swept into the spare bedroom with a flounce, elegantly holding aloft the Champagne flutes. "Ta daaah… You'll never guess what I found in the fridge?" She beamed, smugly.

Daniel sat immobile on the bed, with his back to her.

"Dan?" She froze. Her elation vanished like a puff of smoke, only to be replaced with that old familiar knot in her stomach. She hastily balanced the glasses on the windowsill and saw that Daniel was clutching a scruffy old rucksack. He stared at it, glassy eyed. Grace moved to take it from him and he snatched it away, glaring at her.

"Leave it! Don't…." He snapped.

"what is it?"

He gazed up at his Wife's worried face.

"It's Tom's. These are his things. All the time we were searching for him in London, he must have been here!"

Grace frowned, "But how is that possible? The police followed all leads, spoke to all family members, surely they would have checked…."

"Well they didn't!" He barked.

"OK, but… If his things are here, where is he now?"

They locked eyes and the world shifted suddenly, rolled beneath their feet at the weight of this news which seemed so implausible. Two years ago Daniel's older Brother had vanished. The police put him on the missing persons list, tracked his previous known locations, only to tell the family that it was likely he didn't wish to be found. Or that he was dead. Neither option was acceptable for Daniel and his Mother and they continued to search alone. A long and fruitless search which tore them apart, and almost ended Daniel's marriage.

"What if he's still here somewhere?"

"Dan… "

"I can't ignore this!"

"We'll take this to the Police, they can reopen the investigation."

"Fuck them! They weren't even interested, they never bothered to look properly in the first place."

"Babe, we can't do this again." Grace pleaded.

" We need to let the Police do their job. Maybe they can track him now. If he was in Cornwall the whole time there will be evidence. Someone will know him. They can ask that neighbour we met, that Trenoweth bloke. He'd know something for sure."

Daniel's eyes lit up. "You're right, we need to speak to him…"

"No. Dan, it's not for us to do that. We don't even know him! He might not tell us anything. Please, just let's wait. Just wait and see what the police say." She reached cautiously for the rucksack and this time he let it slip into her hands. She pulled out a change of clothing and a can of deodorant. Nothing to suggest he'd been living here; perhaps only passing through. A small black box had been stuffed into the front pocket. It felt empty and she dropped it onto the bed alongside the pile of clothes. "Are you sure it's his?" She whispered.

Daniel nodded, pointing to a faded old enamel badge of some favourite childhood cartoon animal. "It used to be mine, before he pinched it off me, caused a massive fight and Mum blamed me. I didn't even know he still had it! And I know that t-shirt, he's worn it a million times. It's HIS, Grace. He was HERE and I didn't know… and now he's gone." He closed his eyes, mouth pursed, trying desperately to contain the emotions he refused to allow anyone to see. But Grace knew them only too well. She held him, as she had before, and felt their new life slipping away almost before it had even begun.

CHAPTER 3 - FOUR LANES

Those first weeks in the house were tense, emotions fraught, and tempers flaring when life was meant to have been so much fun. Idyllic even - with endless miles of windswept rugged coastline to explore, wallpaper to be chosen, a Cornish Christmas to plan. But that life was now on hold. Daniel spent numerous hours on the phone to the police, desperately pleading for someone - anyone, to take him seriously. Sleepless nights quickly took their toll and showed in the lines that had carved themselves into his skin; eyes hollow with dark rings beneath. When he wasn't arguing on the phone his hours were spent scouring the house and the internet for more clues as to the whereabouts of his brother. Of which there were none.

Grace had arrived home from shopping one day to hear the tail end of a heated phone conversation between Daniel and his Mum, Janet. Even she was willing, at this point, to let the police handle it, but Daniel had so much unresolved fear and anger, he was taking it out on those around him once more.They spent yet another evening in uncomfortable silence in front of the tv before trudging up to bed.

Grace lay awake in the darkness, every small sound an unwelcome intrusion. She hadn't found it an easy house to settle into and sleep was a fickle bedfellow. The creak of a settling floorboard, the crack of unfamiliar guttering, the thump of a nocturnal visitor landing on the roof all added to her anxiety, one by one.

She tried her best to push them away, but the sounds etched themselves rudely into her awareness. Sleep was still elusive despite the exhaustion that screamed from every muscle within her body. And then, suddenly it was there. A sound that most definitely should not be there. Her eyes snapped open to the darkness. It came again, a scuffle. A thump. Something moved above her, not on the roof, it was closer than that. She listened harder, held her breath until she was blue in the face. It came again, a muffled but unmistakable noise that was not a natural part of the house. She pushed aside the covers and sat up. Tap. Tap... She looked up, the white ceiling a vague grey blur as her eyes slowly adjusted to the dark. Tap tap tap.

"What's wrong?" Daniel mumbled sleepily.

"There's something in the ceiling. I can hear it moving about."

"Probably one of those fecking seagulls on the roof, or a cat or something"

"It's not on the roof, it's in the ceiling. Oh

god... maybe we have rats."

"I'll have a look in the morning, can't do anything now. Ignore it."

Reluctantly she lay back down, pulling the duvet to protect her exposed ear. "How am I supposed to ignore it? So annoying!" She huffed into the pillow. "Horrible creatures." The ceiling gave a further flurry of creaks and thumps in response which sent Grace reaching for some cotton wool to use as makeshift ear plugs. With Daniel's exhausted snores also drowned out she slipped eventually into a restless sleep, filled with sinister dark corners and scurrying shadows.

The next morning when she awoke, Daniel was already on the case. She was pleasantly surprised to see him engaged in something unrelated to his Brother for a change, and brought him a coffee and a croissant. Legs dangled precariously from the square hole in the ceiling as his feet searched for the top rung of the battered old ladder he'd found in the shed. "Coffee's here Dan!"

A muffled "Thanks!" echoed through the ceiling as he struggled back out.

"Can't see any sign of animals up there." He said, gladly sipping the hot drink and ripping the croissant in half to munch on. "No droppings, nests, nothing. It's all pretty clean. Can't see any holes in the roof either, which is good. It's not bats. We'd be screwed if it was. Not allowed to get rid of them. They're protected. Fuck knows why, evil looking things."

"Bats?" Grace shuddered. "Well what was that noise then? Something was up there!"

He shrugged. "Must have been outside. Sounds carry at night. I'll put some traps up there just in case but it'll probably be fine."

Grace wasn't convinced but she didn't feel like having another argument just then.

"Come on," Daniel said, "Let's drive up to the City for a look round. We still need bits for the house and to be honest, I could use a day away from this place." He opened his mouth to speak then closed it again. " I know I've been a complete arse lately. Sorry." He stared dejectedly at his feet. Grace smiled, folding her arms. "That's a bit of an understatement. However... if you buy me lunch and a massive piece of cake... and some new curtains, I might forgive you."

"How about... a pasty, some curtains and a small piece of cake"

"No deal - it's got to be the biggest bit of cake we can find." She smirked. A lady in the supermarket recommended a cafe in Truro that is meant to do THE BEST carrot cake in Cornwall. We should definitely go there first."

Daniel smiled as though a weight had suddenly lifted from his shoulders. "I am sorry though...I know I don't deserve you."

She brushed it off, like she always did, with

a shrug and a smile. Squashing down all the things that would be too painful to ever speak aloud. "I know. I get it. I do." She threw her arms around him and kissed him loudly on the cheek over and over until he had to push her away, laughing. "I love you Grace."

"Love you too, you silly oaf."

They arrived home in the dark. Daniel drove while Grace dozed happily for the first time since the move. They unloaded their new purchases and collapsed on the sofa. It was a bit chilly, but too early for bed, so Daniel lit a fire in the hearth and they snuggled up in front of the tv. Suddenly a log cracked, startling them both. Then came another, louder than the first.

"Is that wood damp?" Grace mumbled.

"Shouldn't be." He leaned forward to poke at the stack of wood and pushed another log in amongst the flames.

The fire dimmed to a soft glow, casting a slightly smoky haze over the room. The hum of the TV, the warmth and crackle of the flames lulled them both into a sleepy trance. Grace fell asleep, head resting on Daniel's shoulder. He kissed the top of her head and smiled.

He stared dreamily into the fire watching the flames leap and curl. It was hypnotic to watch them transform into images, like clouds in the sky, morphing into faces and shapes. Suddenly without warning, a log shifted again, hissing like a serpent as a huge jet of orange flame sent ash flying up into the air. Daniel blinked, eyes wide, as a shadow seemed to lurch out the fire and across the room towards him. Reflexively he jumped, letting out a gasp of surprise, startling Grace from her slumber.

"What happened?"

"Nothing... Shit, that made me jump!" Daniel laughed nervously, patting his chest. "Must get a fire guard next time we're out. Don't want burnt rugs. Come on, I'll damp it down and we can head up to bed. I need to make a start on clearing the garden tomorrow if it's not raining."

As he poked at the hot embers he listened to Grace clattering about in the kitchen. He hadn't been entirely honest with her, in truth he hadn't wanted to scare her, what with all the strange noises, and insomnia she'd been suffering, but he'd seen something tonight in that fire that he could not explain. When that log had popped, sending out smoke and ash, just for a second, he could have sworn the dark shadow flying towards him had a face. And it did not look friendly.

CHAPTER 4 - THE MAGNOLIA TREE

The garden at Fourlanes was a good size, and entirely secluded. It stretched way beyond the rear of the property, surrounded by a high wall on three sides, and a fence bordering a small woodland between them and a quiet street of cottages. At the far end of the garden grew a sprawling magnolia tree. Its branches, currently bare, would within a few months burst into life, smothering the tree in large, velvety white flowers like something from a fairytale.

Sadly the blooms never lasted long, what with the turbulent British weather there was inevitably a storm ready to strip it of petals before it had even finished flowering, but Grace loved magnolias in spite of their fleeting beauty and she was eager to experience her first Cornish spring. She'd awoken again in the early hours and found herself at the window, peering out into the pre-dawn sky. The stark, skeletal form of the tree caught her eye as something moved in the shadows beneath it. Maybe a cat, she wondered - that could also explain the noises on the roof, but no, it couldn't be a cat, it was too tall. Was something climbing the tree? She rubbed her bleary eyes and peered again into the gloom. The shadows shifted and became solid, taking form as her vision cleared.

A person was standing in the garden, staring up at the house.

"Daniel! Quick, wake up! Wake up there's someone in the garden!" She hissed in a panic.

Daniel leapt out of bed, grabbed his dressing gown and raced, still half asleep down the stairs, as Grace followed. He fumbled with the lock and flung open the back door, the security light automatically illuminating the patio in a blinding white beam.

Grace stood shivering behind him. "It was over there, by the tree." She pointed.

He moved in the direction of the magnolia tree, but it was so overgrown with weeds and nettles down there it was impossible to get very close barefoot.

"I don't see anyone now. There's nowhere they could hide in that lot though. Must have legged it round the front. Maybe it's whoever wrote that graffiti on the front wall. Some bored idiot teenagers probably."

"It didn't look like teenagers."

"We'll get some more fencing put up. Come on, get back indoors, it's freezing!"

Jumping back beneath the fading warmth of the duvet, Grace lay there nervously glancing at the window. She couldn't help but feel this dream home was not exactly living up to expectations so far. She snuggled down as Daniel cuddled into her back. He muttered something about it being alright, he'd fix the fencing tomorrow. But she couldn't shake the feeling that it was all very far from being alright.

Daniel fell asleep almost the instant his head hit the pillow. A murky dreamworld filled his vision, blurring the borders between worlds he found himself outside once more. The ground was cold and clammy beneath his naked feet. He stood before a tree. A black tree. It called to him with a soft musical whisper that drew him, almost involuntarily, to stand beneath its leafless branches. He turned, looked up at a house rising out of the darkness, every window burning with a shimmering golden light, and there, right at the top, was a figure in the bedroom window. It was Grace. He wondered why she was up at this late hour, and if she was cold. For some reason his heart felt heavy and sad. He held out his hand, reached up towards her, as five white velvety petals fell into his palm. I'm sorry. He whispered. I'm sorry.

Daniel awoke with a jolt. It was late. The sun burned brightly through the gap in the old beige curtains that didn't quite fit the window. Grace was gone. She'd risen early, not having slept after the night time adventures and she had just given up at 5am and crept quietly downstairs to sit at the kitchen table with her laptop. Daniel found her there at 10am. The kitchen was spotless and the new curtains for the downstairs rooms had been hung. She had bags under her eyes and was on her second cup of coffee. Daniel felt he'd barely slept a wink either, despite the lie in. He rubbed his face and put some bread in the toaster. "We got any bacon?"

Grace nodded. "If you're making a fry up I'll have one. Could use the energy this morning."

He grunted in agreement and grabbed the frying pan.

Grace looked back to her screen, "Hey, I've joined a few local Facebook groups and made a post asking if anyone can keep an eye out for kids coming up here to mess about. Thought it was worth a try. Maybe if people realise the house isn't empty they'll think twice."

Daniel gave another grunt. He hated social media and avoided it like the plague, but it was useful at times.

"Anyway, someone did respond to my post." Continued Grace. "A lady called Ellie, her family have lived in the area for decades apparently. She's a bit of an amateur local historian it seems. She's quite excited to meet us, if you fancy a visitor sometime? She sounds really nice."

"Yeah, why not. Gotta make some friends

sometime."

"She says there's an ancient well nearby with a clootie tree."

"A what?"

"It's where people tie ribbons or wishes or something. It's an ancient ritual."

"Nutters!"

"They're not nutters. I think it's a nice idea. Anyway, it would be cool to have a look. Apparently this whole area has a ton of myths and legends about it. Ellie seems quite into all that."

"Hmmm...."

Grace rolled her eyes at his sarcasm and moved her laptop so he could dish up their breakfast. "Don't be such a misery."

"I'm not. I just don't believe in all that hokey pokey nonsense as you well know."

"Oh I know Mr grumpy, I know!" She smirked.

"Changing the subject, " Daniel coughed. "I thought you'd be more upset about last night."

"Well I'm not happy about it, but what else can I do?"

"I'll get a bit of fencing later and see if we can make it more secure. Maybe we should get a guard dog or something."

Grace shot him a stern warning look.

"Electric fence?" He continued. "OK, OK... just trying to cheer you up. Just the plain old wooden fencing then. Maybe a bit of razor wire for the top."

"I'm tired. Don't test me. You on the other hand slept like a baby! Again! Wish I knew how you do it."

"I didn't. I had a really weird dream, more like a nightmare." Daniel frowned as he recalled the disturbing imagery. "I was down by the tree, only it was black, like burnt or something, there was this weird noise, like whispering, and I saw you looking at me from the bedroom window. I kept thinking how cold you must be, and there was something else… can't quite remember." He ruffled his hair.

Grace chewed her toast and stared at him. "That is creepy."

He pressed knuckles into his temples in an attempt to rub away the headache that had

begun to form there. " Ah… load of bollocks! It's just stress. Hey, maybe that's what we should do, burn the thing down and pave it all over."

Grace finished her breakfast in silence. It wasn't like Daniel to even remember his dreams, much less talk about them. And this particular one, for some reason, sent an unpleasant shiver down her spine.

CHAPTER 5 - DARKNESS FALLS

Daniel dragged himself into town, leaving Grace to finish hanging the curtains. He wandered the DIY shop in a daze, still groggy. Fencing purchased, he headed home. Unloading the car, he could see Grace inside, sitting at the table with her laptop again. For some reason this annoyed him. Bloody Facebook. The last thing they needed were nosey snoopers trying to befriend them. He slammed the boot and she barely glanced up.

He dragged the wood and tools round the back and angrily threw them into the weeds. Then he kicked the tree trunk just for good measure. Stupid bloody fence idea. He didn't believe there'd been someone in the garden anyway. Why would they bother? It was just Grace's overactive imagination. And now he had even more work to do. He grumbled and cursed to himself, pulled on his gardening gloves and grabbed the spade. He had no idea why his mood was so bleak today, but he could feel his last nerve start to fray.

The fence proved awkward to install, as expected, but he persevered. He would rather stay outside in the cold until it was done, even if it took all night, than go indoors and pretend he could have any semblance of a normal conversation. Even once the fence was complete he found himself pulling up weeds and looking for something to cut down, or dig up, purely for something to keep him occupied.

Grace had popped her head out of the door earlier and pulled a face at his gruff refusal at a cup of tea. He hadn't seen her again, and nor would he. She was busy painting woodwork in the bathroom now.

He ripped vigorously at the sea of nettles beneath the magnolia tree, gradually clearing the muddy patch of rough ground. It was probably never going to be beautiful, but at least it would no longer resemble a derelict building site. With a grunt he tore at the last few weeds and stopped suddenly. There, firmly embedded in the soft ground was the unmistakable imprint of a shoe. His thoughts swam. Shit! There was no way he was going to tell Grace. He couldn't. She'd be up all night keeping watch. It would make her paranoid. It would be his fault, everything's always his fault. It was his fault they moved there in the first place, and now she'd want to move back to London. No. He wouldn't tell her. Large raindrops began to fall, slowly at first, then faster. Pitter patter on the muddy ground. He stuck out his foot and smeared the edge of the footprint, paused a moment, then smeared the rest of it. There. Now it had never even existed. The rain fell more heavily now, droplets clinging to his hair and face but he barely noticed.

Something tickled his cheek and buzzed annoyingly. He swatted at his ear and flicked away a large, fat fly. Disgusting thing. He shuddered, removing his gloves. Must have been hidden in the weeds, or more likely living on some dead thing. He glanced apprehensively about and sniffed, but to his relief, found nothing. The buzzing grew louder, and a second fly landed on the back of his hand. He flapped it away, throwing the gloves onto the pile of gardening tools and stomped towards the house.

Pain zigzagged through his temples as another headache began, they were almost daily now. Kicking off his boots he stumbled indoors and collapsed onto the sofa. He rubbed his eyelids and forehead with muddy hands, as if that would do any good. It didn't. Staring up at the ceiling he wondered if he was coming down with the flu. If he just sat still for a while maybe he'd feel better.

"Dan? Are you OK?"

He jumped. "Eh? I didn't know you were there."

Grace pursed her lips, sucked in a breath through her teeth.

That really pissed him off. "Why are you glaring at me for fuck sake? You made me jump, that's all."

"We've been speaking for the last five minutes."

Daniel scowled, dredging his mind for any recollection of a conversation. There was none. He stared blankly at the annoyed woman in the doorway, not entirely certain if he were actually awake or just dreaming again.

"I asked if you could clean up all the mud you walked in, you were a bit blunt, but you definitely muttered something. You couldn't have been talking in your sleep as your eyes were open. You looked at me!"

"What did I say?" He sulked.

She sighed. "It doesn't matter. I think you should probably have an early night though. Maybe you're ill. You're definitely exhausted. I'll clean up, it's fine."

He rubbed his forehead again, struggling to focus his thoughts. A small thread of anger was still there, bubbling just beneath the surface. Suddenly it ignited. "There's nothing wrong with me!" He blurted. "Why does there always have to be something wrong with me? Why is it always my fault? And stop whining about a bit of mud... I was out there trying to keep YOU happy!"

"What are you talking about? What's your fault?"

"Just stop it.. Stop it Grace, I've had enough!"

"Enough of what? I don't understand what's upset you". She reached for his arm but he lurched to his feet, swaying as he did so. Whispers taunted him, voices in the room - he whipped his head around to find noone there. A dark shadow on the wall moved, the light dimming for a brief second. Did Grace see that too?

"Dan, please just come and lie down. I'll get you some paracetamol, you need to sleep."

"I don't want to sleep and I don't want any fucking paracetamol. I can't deal with any more of this crap! It's one thing after another with you isn't it? First it's my Brother, now the house is a problem. I'm not even supposed to care that my Brother vanished into thin air and no one gives a shit where he is, but if I try to find him? Well I'm just doing it wrong aren't I?"

"That's not fair. We ALL care about Tom. And we all tried to help find him."

"You didn't even want to! And then we moved here and found more evidence and you didn't want me to keep looking. Just brush it all under the carpet, he's gone and that's that."

Grace recoiled in shock. "I know you're hurting, but don't take it out on me. I did want you to find him, I told you to give the new evidence to the police."

"For all the good that did! They can't even be bothered to get off their fat arses and come round to check it out!"

Grace tried again to pacify him but he wasn't

having any of it. He continued to rant.

"...and you never wanted to come here anyway did you? You hate the place. You've hated it since we arrived. You moan about the state of the garden, and the decorating, you don't sleep and there's noises, and people in the garden... well, you'll be glad to know at least that IS true!"

Grace froze. "What do you mean?"

"I found footprints under the tree, so it looks like you're right and I'm wrong yet again! Bet that makes you happy now!"

"Footprints? No, that does NOT make me happy Daniel. Were you even going to tell me?"

"No. I didn't want to worry you even more, but of course I'm just the selfish git who thinks about no one else right? I'm just the cause of all our troubles. I probably caused your miscarriage too and killed our baby, just because I'm the arsehole who's ruined your life. Right?"

Grace turned pale, her voice trembled. "How dare you say something like that? I don't know what's wrong with you, but I am sick of trying to pick up the pieces every time you have a meltdown. You can sort it out by yourself from now on. I'm done with this conversation."

Without another word she ran upstairs. He heard her sobbing as the bedroom door closed. She couldn't even bring herself to slam it. That was Grace all over. Never raised her voice, never even swore in public, but he'd pushed her too far this time and he didn't even understand why.

CHAPTER 6 - MR BLACKTHORN

Daniel slammed the front door behind him and stomped off towards the village. It was dark, windy and cold, but at least the rain had stopped, leaving in its wake a glistening sparkle of streetlights reflected in the pavements and puddles on the road. A pungent waft of coal fires added its own layer to the heavy atmosphere blanketing Penmerryn tonight. The tide was high and it was forecast to be a wild one. No doubt he'd have the Wreckers Inn to himself this evening, as more sensible folk preferred to head straight home on a night like this.

Once inside the pub he leaned against the bar and let the warmth seep into his bones. He sighed miserably. The fire that had burned so intensely in his chest a short while ago had now fizzled, pathetically, and he felt like the biggest and stupidest asshole on the planet.

Ordering a pint he pulled out his phone, intending to call Grace and apologise, but a curiously familiar sound, like a breath or a whisper caught his attention. Looking over his shoulder, he saw a man seated by the fire. An odd sort of fellow, balding, with eyes a touch too small. He was thin and gangly, giving the appearance that his clothes belonged to someone else and didn't quite fit properly. The man nodded and waved him over as though he were greeting an old friend. Daniel, not normally keen to make conversation with strangers, found himself scooping up his pint and moving to sit opposite the beady eyed chap.

"Evening." He muttered.

"Good evening to you too." The man replied with a strange chirpy lilt.

Daniel couldn't tell if the man was smiling politely at him or just smirking.

"What a night to be out and about!" The man said. "The first of many. This Winter will be a bad one, mark my words."

Daniel raised an eyebrow. "What makes you say that? I was led to believe winters are pretty mild in the south west."

"They can be indeed, but don't be fooled. There have been some truly terrible storms on these shores." The man sipped his drink and smirked some more, and Daniel considered excusing himself to another table. He really wanted to call Grace, but before he could open his mouth, the man spoke again.

"Mr Blackthorn, to my friends." He offered an unpleasantly bony, outstretched hand, which Daniel shook, somewhat hesitantly.

"Err... Daniel." He stuttered in reply.

Mr Blackthorn continued. "Daniel eh? I hear you're new to the village. How are you and your lovely wife getting on?"

Daniel was lost for words. "Oh... I... we're good thanks."

"Word travels in a small place like this. Everyone knows everyone's business." Mr Blackthorn snickered. "Welcome to West Cornwall. Home of the giants, piskies, the knockers, and the merfolk..."

"I'm not much of a believer in all that I'm afraid, but the scenery is pretty nice." Daniel muttered despondently into his beer.

"Ah a sceptic! Next you'll be telling me you've never seen a ghost, and you don't believe in Santa claus." He laughed heartily at his own words. It was an uncomfortable sound, his laughter. Something in its tone and pitch sent a chill though Daniel that made his bones grate.

He began to wonder why he'd joined this strange man in the first place, and downed his pint as quickly as he knew how, hoping that it would signal his excuse to leave, but Mr Blackthorn continued on, seemingly oblivious, or perhaps just ignoring the obvious. "If it's scenery you're looking for I can recommend some exceptionally lovely places. From lonely and windswept cliff tops to charming villages, or beaches, Cornwall has some of the best coastline in the world you know!"

"I have to confess, I haven't done too much

research. Wouldn't mind a good walk along the cliffs though." Daniel pondered.

"You'll be wanting to get yourself over to Botallack then, not too far from here. A perfect way to blow away some cobwebs and enjoy some Cornish history."

"Botallack, that's where the tin mine ruins are, isn't it?"

"Indeed it is. Lonely and wild up there, or Lamorna with its woodland valley and rugged cove. Such a pity it hasn't been better taken care of, but still, peaceful nonetheless. So much to see in this wonderful County, but personally I love the moors, where you can walk for hours and not see another soul."

"Yeh, I must admit that does sound pretty tempting right now. Being able to not see another person for hours is almost unheard of where I'm from." Daniel grudgingly agreed.

"And where is that?" Mr Blackthorn asked, a gleam in his eye.

"London."

"The big City! Ghastly place, you're better off away from it."

"Where are you from?" Asked Daniel.

"Originally? I'm a man of the North. The wilds of Northumbria and the Scottish borders. Ah the hills and mountains of the old country… I do miss them. God's Country, they call it." He laughed to himself. Daniel wasn't entirely sure what was funny.

"When did you move to Cornwall?" Dan continued, not wanting to seem rude.

"Too many years ago to count. The old places though, they're no longer recognisable." He sneered as though recalling some old unpleasant memory. "Stones and hills that belong to no one but the earth. Folks think it belongs to them now, but they'll realise one day. One day they'll see the old power again. It's never gone, but lies dormant you see. Beneath the ground. Always watching." He chuckled.

Daniel began to wonder if he was somehow older than he looked, and maybe a bit senile, or perhaps just a little on the eccentric side. He did smell a little musty. Daniel wondered briefly what sort of conditions the man lived in. Perhaps a damp little cottage, or worse, a squalid bedsit. No one deserved that, no matter how odd they were.

Mr Blackthorn paid him no attention, seeming to enjoy the sound of his own voice. "I travelled on to Kernow, many moons since. A special place it is, full of power. Dark, ancient and unpredictable. Or dull, for those who manage to avoid old Keldd." He set about chuckling again with a raspy cough like an old man who'd smoked his entire life.

"Kernow? What's that?" Daniel queried.

Full of self importance, and clearly enjoying having an audience, Mr Blackthorn enlightened him. "Kernow is the old name for Cornwall. Comes from the celtic word for 'headland', spoken in a tongue almost forgotten now. The language of the witch we used to call it. Used to be plenty o' them in these old hills." He winked.

Daniel stifled a laugh. "Witches? Think we're a bit past that aren't we?"

"Ah you can scoff young Daniel, but wise folk know better. In places like these you can find them still, hidden in plain sight. Going about their business. Conjuring the spirits of old."

"I don't believe in ghosts and all that nonsense. And Keldd, is that another celtic word for something?"

Mr Blackthorn sat back, with his arms crossed. His piercing gaze made Daniel feel almost queasy. In spite of his comedic appearance, the odd little smile on his lips did not reach his eyes, and his intense stare had something resembling that of a dead animal.

"Keldd is a name as old as time itself. It belongs to no one and nowhere, and yet that is what some may call me. But what of your lovely wife? Is she more open minded to the supernatural?"

"My Wife? Well, she….umm."

"What do you believe in, Daniel?" He whispered suddenly, lurching across the table.

Daniel stammered again, feeling defensive, unsure how such a conversation had even begun, and even less sure how to end it. "I don't know… The real world. Things I can see and touch. Real life."

"Ah but what of the mysteries? You must have some of those too. The things you can't find an explanation for. What of them?"

"Just because I don't have an answer yet, doesn't mean I won't find one."

Mr Blackthorn had found a loose thread, and tugged on it ever so gently. "Sounds like you have something on your mind? Something you seek... something specific you need to get off your chest?"

Daniel felt a spark reignite inside him, like the grind of a match against red phosphorus and powdered glass and he spit out words that he would never have spoken otherwise. "Yes. Yes there is if you must know. My brother went missing and the Police think he's dead. My Wife thinks I should give up, but I know differently. I know he came to Cornwall and if he's still here, I'll find him!"

Mr Blackthorn leaned in closer, a sudden spark of interest giving the illusion of life to his dead eyed stare. "Well now, I'm sorry to hear that. What makes you think he's here?"

"I found some of his belongings in my Uncle's house. I didn't even know he was in touch with Uncle John, but apparently he came down here for some reason without telling anyone."

"Hmmm... Uncle John. Good old Uncle John of Fourlanes. The crossroads on the hill."

Daniel stared back at the man, dumbstruck. "You knew him?"

"Oh yes. Honest man. He always kept his word."

"Kept his word? Hang on, can I get you another drink?" Daniel desperately needed this conversation to continue. His curiosity was piqued.

Mr Blackthorn flashed a toothy grin. "Well now, that would be very welcome, thank you." He nodded.

Daniel returned from the bar with two pints, he set them down, now fully invested in quizzing this man about his Uncle, and perhaps he'd even seen Tom? Perhaps this would prove to be the most useful lead yet.

"So you were saying... John, how well did you know him?"

"Well enough. Nice fellow, a man of his word. He was a believer in the ancient ways you know? He knew it was a mistake to meddle. He knew the consequences."

Daniel frowned. "Meddle? What do you mean by that? Did you see him with a younger man, at all? Looks similar to me, light brown hair, blue eyes, 5'8", leather jacket?"

"Your brother, I presume?"

Daniel nodded eagerly.

"I don't recall... I might have, but old John made himself scarce in recent times. Didn't like to leave the house much."

"Why not?"

Mr Blackthorn shrugged. "Who can say? P'raps he fell out with someone."

Frustrating little man! Daniel started to feel like he was being strung along.

"This brother of yours. Close, were you?"

"Yes. Fairly."

"He didn't tell you he was off though?"

Daniel scowled. "We used to be close. Then he got involved with some friends that probably weren't so great for him. He... he became secretive. Stopped coming to visit and then... he just vanished."

"So why the desperation to find him? He was old enough to do as he pleased, and didn't care to keep in touch."

"He's my Brother. He would do the same for me."

"Would he? I wonder. Tell me Daniel, what lengths would you go to, to find him?"

"What do you mean?"

"Well, hypothetically." Blackthorn shrugged again, pint glass gripped between his scrawny hands. "How far would you go? How badly do you want to find your Brother?"

"It's not a joking matter. I'd do anything to find him, of course I would!"

"All I'm saying is, what if someone could help you? What would you give in a fair exchange? What if all you had to do was buy a man a drink?" Mr Blackthorn shrugged, utterly un-flustered.

Daniel's anger flared. "What are you trying

to say? I'm sorry but I just think you're taking the piss now, it's not a joking matter. If you know something you need to tell me now!"

Mr Blackthorn held up his hand. "Now now, no need to take offence, I was only takin' an interest. I tell you what, I'll have a think, and ask around for you. See if I can't find out something. Plenty o' folks around these parts know what's what. If your Brother's here I'm sure someone knows."

Daniel felt his cheeks begin to burn again and excused himself, fleeing to the toilets. He berated himself for speaking so freely with a complete stranger! And a stranger that seemed to know who he was, at that! He returned shortly, a little calmer, but still confused, to an empty table. He slumped dejectedly back into his chair to finish his pint and spotted beneath the glass a folded piece of paper. It was just a promotional flyer from a local band, there were stacks of them littering the main bar. But there was, however, something scribbled in biro on the back, now partially smudged with condensation from his glass.

It looked to be a somewhat crudely drawn map with directions to a place called Carn Madrow, and it was signed Happy hunting! Blackthorn. Daniel snatched it up and took his empty glass over to the bar. He nodded to the bartender. "Hey, have you heard of Carn Madrow?"

The young man looked thoughtful. "Can't

say I have. I've not been down here long though. Moved down from Plymouth a few months ago." He peered at the scrap of paper Daniel held up. "There's plenty of old stones and odd things out on the moors though, if that's where you're going."

Daniel folded the piece of paper and shoved it into his pocket. "Maybe. That bloke I was with was telling me about places to visit. Just wondered if it was worth a trip out. Is he a local?"

The barman wrinkled his nose as though he'd caught a whiff of something gone bad. "I don't exactly know. Nobody does. He shows up in here occasionally. Bit of an oddball. Wouldn't take what he says at face value to be honest. Seems a bit of a weasley sort if you ask me."

"Fair enough, I thought the same to be honest. Anyway, thanks for the drink, you'll be seeing me a fair bit, my Wife and I just moved into the village. Up at Fourlanes."

The man's eyebrow twitched at the word Fourlanes. "Ah, nice. Welcome to Penmerryn!"

Daniel awaited the inevitable flurry of newcomer questions, but they never came, so, taking the hint, he excused himself and set off for home.

Daniel plodded anxiously up the drive, full of regret, noting that the house was shrouded in darkness. He put his key in the lock and the door creaked open. Well she hasn't changed the locks, that was a good sign at least.

"Grace?" He called hopefully, up the stairs. "I'm back… and I'm sorry!"

The silence was deafening. He continued up the stairs in the darkness, a soft yellow glow radiated from beneath the bedroom door. He tapped lightly before pushing it open a crack. "Grace? I'm really sorry. Please. I don't know what happened earlier." Grace lay in bed, tucked beneath the duvet with her back to him as she pretended to be engrossed in a book. He hesitated before cautiously seating himself on the bed beside her. "I probably don't deserve forgiveness do I? I just don't know what happened to me… I… felt so weird. Like I wasn't myself. It was like, I was outside my body watching someone else saying all that shit. It's no excuse I know, but…" He dropped his head into his hands.

"I've never seen you like that." Grace said quietly,.

"Maybe I am ill. Maybe it's stress or something. I don't know."

"We'll get you registered at the local doctors and see what they say. I've already been up there, they seem nice enough."

He nodded, silently resigned to doing whatever was necessary to turn things around. Because apparently moving three hundred miles to a new home in a new County wasn't enough to fix things.

"Where did you go?" She asked, putting her book down and rolling over to face him. Her eyes were red and puffy, he noted guiltily.

"Umm, the pub. Was going to call you as soon as I got there but… "

"Hmm…"

"No, I was! I just…" For some reason he couldn't quite bring himself to relay the events of this evening and his encounter with the crazy old man. It all seemed like nonsense now anyway. What did some weird old bloke know about his brother? Nothing. Even the bar staff didn't know who he was. He'd been taken in by the local loon, something else to be proud of tonight. Grace didn't need to know about that either.

CHAPTER 7 - THINGS THAT ARE HIDDEN

Determined to make things right, Daniel kept to his word and the following day, drove into town to find Nansdean Surgery. He spent an uncomfortable hour filling in forms and providing 'samples' and then somehow managed to speak to a somewhat hurried, if apologetic female GP, who checked his blood pressure and recommended he try some herbal stress remedies before returning in a few weeks to see how he was getting on. It was better than nothing, and if it made Grace happy, then he'd put up with it. He'd walk through fire for that woman and all she did for him.

Saturday arrived, a day heralded with sunshine and blue skies, it was almost springlike. Feeling reinvigorated after the heaviness of the previous week, Daniel suggested a road trip. A day exploring all the local beauty spots just like they'd planned. The smile on his Wife's face had spoken volumes as he proudly presented her with a Sainsburys carrier bag full of picnic supplies, two pairs of cheap, silly looking sunglasses, a beach towel, and a brightly illustrated tourist map he'd found by the checkout.

She rolled her eyes, giggling. "So where are we off to today, Indiana Jones?"

"Well I thought we could see if this St Michael's Mount is worth a visit, and maybe a drive down through Penzance and Mouse Hole. Someone told me Lamorna cove is nice, we can follow the map round the coast and see where we end up?"

Grace doubled over laughing.

"What's so funny? I thought you'd love it!"

She snorted through her words. "I do... it's just, it's not called Mouse Hole... it's pronounced Mouwzle."

He huffed."How am I meant to know that? stupid Cornish spellings. How do you know anyway?"

"Ellie told me. Everyone gets it wrong the first time, that and Marazion... it's Marra-zyon."

"I can see we've got a way to go before we fit in round here." He grumbled. "Best get going and piss off the locals with our stupid foreign ways then."

With Daniel in the driving seat, they set off in the direction of Mount's Bay. First stop, the picturesque little market town of Marazion. Grace gasped as they drove into the bay, the tide was out, but their entire view was dominated by the magical vision that was St Michaels' mount. A majestic medieval castle perched atop a tiny rocky island, and connected to the mainland by a cobbled causeway that would be completely submerged at high tide. It was straight out of a fairy tale. "Wow! I'd heard of it but never imagined it was so beautiful!" Grace cooed. "Hurry up and park, just look at that beach!"

Daniel laughed. Happy to see Grace so excited. "Alright alright, hold your horses! It does look pretty impressive I'll admit."

"No wonder Cornwall has so many legends, with inspiration like this. Ellie sent me a link to this website with all the old stories of smugglers and giants, and mermaids, and stone circles. There's one near us called Carn Madrow, and Men an Tol. We have to go and see those too!"

"Carn Madrow? I've heard of that one. Did it say any more about it?" Daniel tried not to sound too interested, but couldn't help but wonder, as he navigated the tight corner that led into a car park right on the seafront.

"Hmm, can't remember. Something about the devil or dancing demons or something. Anyway, there's also a legend that says a giant lived on this Island, oh, and Archangel Michael appeared to fishermen here at the castle, and that's why it's named after him, and he also fought the devil who was carrying a stone to block the gates of hell. I believe that's why Helston is named Hell stone."

"Why, because it's the gateway to hell?"

Daniel snickered.

"No... it's where he dropped the stone. I think. Or maybe it was somewhere else. Oh I don't know."

"Slow down, jeez, anyone would think this was all historical fact." He snorted disdainfully.

"Well there's no harm in being open minded."

"Open minded?" He guffawed. "It's kids stuff. No such things as angels and devils and giants."

"Well why were you so interested in the stone circle then?" She bit back, impatiently.

"I just heard it was a nice place for a picnic. Someone mentioned it in the pub. That's all."

Grace ignored him. She was used to his lack of imagination, and turned her attention back to photographing the castle. They made their way up from the carpark and through the narrow winding streets to the very top of the hill where they could breathe deeply the raw scent of the sea air. Grace felt as though she stood at the very top of the world overlooking such an expanse of blue, softly buffeted by the wind. It was like freedom personified. She closed her eyes and felt every muscle in her body relax.

Crossing the road, they made their way back down towards the castle, enjoying glimpses of the craggy mount and cerulean sea from little hidden viewpoints down secret alleyways and narrow lanes along the way. Once back down at sea level they eagerly ventured out onto the grainy golden sand that curved for miles around Mounts Bay, with the bustling towns of Penzance and Newlyn in the distance. A path of neatly laid cobbles cut through the rock pools and seaweed to the mount itself, and from there opened up into a small harbour, surrounded by victorian granite cottages and lush tropical gardens. The majestic grey rock rose up before them with a winding path to the top, and the castle, once a Priory, seemed to hover somewhere in the clouds above. Not hard to see why there would be talk of angels here.

Sadly today the castle itself was closed for the winter, and there would be no trek up the cliffside, but Grace was enamoured and longed to return.

"Can you imagine the views from inside?" She squeaked excitedly. "Oh we have to come back in the spring."

Daniel peered up. It was a lot more effort than it seemed from the mainland that's for sure. "You can probably see right round the headland on a clear day from up there. Yeah, we'll come back when it's open, there's a nice looking restaurant over there too. Your birthday is in April." He winked.

Her eyes lit up as she nodded happily.

"Oh well… I suppose we should get back to the car and see what we can find next." He continued.

"Probably not anything as good as this." Grace reluctantly dragged herself away from the dreamy little island and back to the car.

The remainder of the day flew past, and by 5pm they'd earned the right to call themselves fully fledged tourists. The huge cream tea they'd rapidly consumed on a pit stop by the harbour in Porthleven, had long since worn off and now the local fish and chip shop had their names written all over it. Grace flopped into an armchair, plate heavy with food, balanced on her lap while Dan parked himself on the sofa with a cushion for a tray.

"God this smells good, I'm so hungry!" Grace drooled eagerly.

"It's hard work having fun." He chuckled through a mouthful of battered cod. "You've even caught the sun, you know."

Suddenly Grace let out a rather explosive sneeze and nearly toppled the plate. Shortly after came another one. She grimaced. "Uh oh... maybe a bit too much fresh sea air. Tell me I'm not coming down with something, please. I do feel exhausted."

They finished their meal amid a flurry of sneezes, and Grace decided that a shower and an early night was needed. Daniel agreed as he cleared the dishes.

"You go up, I'll watch telly for a bit and let you sleep."

"That's big of you." She smirked. "You've got that new bottle of whisky to keep you company too."

"Oooh.. yes! Want a hot toddy to take up with you?"

"Nah. I'll give it a miss thanks." She leaned over to kiss him on the cheek. "Don't stay up too late."

"I won't."

Sunday rolled around and Daniel left Grace sleeping to creep downstairs. He'd not long been abed, to be fair. He'd managed to binge watch a new Netflix series with the help of a few whisky and cokes, then after nodding off on the sofa for an hour he crawled upstairs for a few more hours of fitful sleep. The nightmares were getting worse. Such surreal dreams that always ended with him waking in a sweat. He shuddered and tried to push the memory away.

He kicked his heels restlessly for a while. What he really wanted to do was check out the attic again, but he didn't want to wake Grace. He poked his head around the bedroom door. She was a softly snoring lump beneath the duvet and he lingered a moment, before closing the door and creeping back downstairs. He halted outside the spare room. They hadn't yet done much with it since the discovery of Tom's belongings. He pushed the door open and blinked uncomfortably as a beam of sunlight caught him right in the eye.

Putting up a hand to shield his eyes, he drew one half of the curtains and looked aimlessly around the room. Tom's bag lay on the bed, contents still in a pile beside it. He shook out the t-shirt then folded it neatly, placing it back on the bed. He wondered if it shouldn't really go in the wardrobe. I mean, that's where clothes ought to be stored right? He opened the door, scooped up the t-shirt and stashed it on a shelf. He did the same with the rest of Tom's clothes and carefully set the can of deodorant and wash bag next to them. The interior of the wardrobe smelt a bit stale, like it hadn't been used for a really long time. Grace would put some sort of air freshener thing in there, but Tom would hate his clothes to end up stinking of lavender.

Daniel stared at them for the longest time. It was such a futile effort. Why was he pretending that Tom was even coming back for them? They ought to just go in the bin. Shouldn't they? What kind of idiot folds a dead man's clothes and puts them away.

"He's not dead!" Dan muttered under his breath. "He's not fucking dead, I know it."

He reached for the backpack and absently picked at the badge pinned to its pocket. The enamel was so worn you could hardly make out the image. Where are you Tom? Placing the bag inside the wardrobe, with Tom's clothes, he noticed the box that still lay on the bed. It was fairly ordinary, not too heavy. No labels, no embossing, just a plain box which was small enough to fit in the palm of his hand. He toyed with it, looking for a way to open it, but there was none.

He couldn't quite place what was so strange about it at first, but then he realised it was the colour. It was black. Sure, but there's black and then there's black. Anything printed or painted has a sheen to it, some kind of reflective quality, but this did not. It was as though it were made from shadow. The darkest, blackest shadow. The kind of shadow that seems to absorb light and dark almost as if it were a giant black hole sucking in space and stars and solar systems and all the life in the universe.That kind of black.

Daniel recalled his dream about the magnolia tree. The tree had been that kind of black. He shook the thought away and stuffed the box hurriedly inside the bag, firmly shutting the wardrobe door.

His eyes were then drawn to the fireplace, or rather, the replastered section of wall where the fireplace should have been. He gave the wall a tap with his knuckles, then again. It gave a hollow echo. Why bother sealing it up? He wondered. The room was large enough to accommodate it, and the chimney was sound. It would be nice to have an attractive fireplace in the spare room, be more homely for guests. He gave the plaster another rap, but harder this time. Curiosity was beginning to get the better of him, and he knew what Grace would say, there's plenty of more important things to be getting on with than knocking down walls, but he really wanted to know what was behind that plaster.

He marched off to retrieve his tool box from a corner of the kitchen, and picked up a large hammer. Nope, no good. That would make too much noise and bring an angry wife into the picture. He swapped it for an old wooden handled screwdriver and a much smaller hammer, then, placing the tip of the screwdriver against the plaster he gave it a little tap. Flimsy plaster cracked and flaked away from the small hole he'd made. Oh well, might as well keep going now, he thought. More taps. More plaster crumbled. The hole quickly became large enough to fit a hand inside and he crouched to peer in but it was too dark and dirty to make anything out.

Just then he heard the creak of floorboards above and he did not want Grace to know about his excavations just yet. He brushed the mess of plaster on the carpet into a pile and grabbed a large picture off the wall propping the frame against the wall to cover the damage. If she looked in the room now he could say he was rehanging the pictures. He pushed his tools under the bed, closed the door and nipped quietly down stairs. He boiled the kettle, pretending to busy himself, but Grace did not appear. He considered going back to the fireplace, but decided against it. She might not be sleeping anymore and he couldn't risk being discovered. Daniel decided instead to hang the new pictures they'd bought for the lounge and hallway, then, discovering they were out of milk, he drove to the supermarket for a quick restock and grabbed a bouquet of flowers while he was there. Grace loved fresh flowers in the house, especially lilies.

Two hours later and the jobs were done, Daniel sat twiddling his thumbs. He glanced out of the window and remembered the graffiti. One bucket of soapy water and a scrubbing brush later, and he was finding the paint more difficult to remove from the pock marked granite than he'd imagined. Rubbing his sweaty brow with his forearm he grumbled away to himself.

"Alright there?"

Daniel jumped, feeling equal parts annoyed, and embarrassed to be caught talking to himself. It was the man they'd met on their first day here, what was his name again?

"Oh, hello! Err... Terry isn't it?"

"Aye, tis. Just thought I'd drop by and see how you're getting on. P'raps you might fancy coming up for a cuppa sometime."

"Ah, right. Well, thanks but Grace isn't very well at the moment. Still got tons of work to do, the house is keeping us pretty busy."

"So I see." Terry nodded towards the soaking

mess between them. "Know what that is, do ya?"

Daniel grimaced, he really wasn't in the mood for chit chat. "Bloody local kids messing about. Only just got the chance to clean it off. Hey, you haven't seen any of them hanging around have you?"

Terry shook his head. "Not the sort of thing that usually happens round here. Got good kids in this village, from decent families."

"Well not all of them, apparently!" Daniel snapped. "And you might want to mention the fact that we're keeping an eye out for whoever it is we've seen lurking in the garden at night too. No doubt those same good kids from the village."

"Well now, I don't think anyone will take too kindly to accusations, but if I hear of anything…"

"You do that!" Daniel was feeling angrier by the minute and wishing this nosey old coot would just take the hint and leave. He dumped the scrubbing brush into the bucket with a splash and made his excuses before stomping back inside. Grace stood in the kitchen, hands on her hips.

Daniel ground to a halt. " I didn't know you were up. How are you feeling?"

"A bit better. Why were you so rude to our neighbour?"

"What? I wasn't."

"The window's open, I heard you."

"I wasn't rude. I was just busy trying to scrub that crap off. And then he starts getting all funny when I suggested it was some local kids. I mean, who else would it be?" He grumbled.

Grace sighed and eased herself into a chair. "Nice flowers." She nodded towards the vase.

"I thought they might cheer you up." He muttered hopefully. "I finished putting up the pictures too."

She tried to look pleased. "Thank you. I'm just tired. What was all the racket about earlier?"

"Racket? Sorry, probably just me putting up the pictures?"

"No, it sounded like you were in the spare room."

He shrugged and shook his head emphatically.

Grace rolled her eyes. "Whatever. I might go back to bed actually, still feeling a bit wobbly. Did you get some more tissues?"

"Yeah, I'll bring them up for you with a cup of tea. I'll get back to that graffiti…" He offered, shooing her from the room with a quick glance outside to make sure Terry was long gone.

With Grace safely returned to her sick bed he peeked out the window again. What are all those weird symbols? He muttered to himself. He spied Grace's laptop, still open, on the table. She never bothered closing it, or logging off. It was a terrible habit that Daniel berated her for. What if she left it somewhere and the wrong person got into her accounts? He was always complaining. And yet, here he was, sliding into her seat and casually scrolling through her Facebook page, with one eye on the door.

There were a ton of messages from this 'Ellie'. He scanned a few with interest. She seemed a bit over-excitable when it came to the 'woo woo stuff', but otherwise alright.

He clicked open a new tab and started a search for satanic symbols. A page of random images loaded in. Mostly your standard stuff - pentagrams and various tattoo designs, but on the 3rd page something caught his eye. It was similar to a pentagram, but with some added swirls and what appeared to be foreign writing in a triangle. He shifted in his seat to peer outside at the graffiti, yes, it was definitely similar.

He clicked on the image to bring up the web page it was on. An old chat forum discussing paganism and ancient symbology. Most of the conversation went over his head, although he had heard of Aleister Crowley and his odd reputation, but just as he was losing interest and about to close the page, he spied an old post from ten years ago that for some reason piqued his interest. It was a short post, with a couple of photographs attached, and the post itself had only three replies. The photos were of a wall covered in graffiti. Daniel clicked to enlarge the picture. There it was. The same symbol that was outside his house, on a wall somewhere in Newcastle. He sat back, astounded. The post read:

"Can anyone help me find out what this means?

This symbol keeps popping up wherever I seem to go and I don't know why, or who is putting it there. I'm sure someone is just trying to freak me out but I also had a letter in the post which had this symbol in it."

Daniel realised he'd been holding his breath, he let it out slowly, feeling lightheaded. He continued to read. The first two replies had nothing to offer but advice on stalking, however the third was more intriguing..

"Hi, it looks like you've been targeted. They don't mess about. If I were you I'd ignore it and don't accept anything from anybody until it stops. It happened to someone I knew once. Be careful who you speak to!"

Daniel's heart raced. Targeted? He thought back to the strange noises and the figure in the garden. Shit! Those village kids were clearly into something a bit heavier than just causing mischief. He searched through to see if the original poster's account was accessible, it wasn't, not without being logged in. Daniel hurriedly went through the process of creating an account and logging in, then he found a button that would allow him to send a fellow user a message. It was ten years old though, what were the chances that this guy was still using the same email address? Slim but he'd have to take a chance. He bashed out a message:

"Hey. Hope you're still receiving messages from this forum, but I really need to ask you some questions about that symbol you mentioned. What happened

to the person you know who was targeted? Who was doing it and why? I think someone I know may have been having the same issue. Thanks in advance, Dan"

He reopened the image file and right clicked to save it to the laptop and bookmarked the web page. It was the only information he had and he wasn't going to lose it.

That night, Daniel's dreams were filled with strange faceless people, hiding down alleyways. Every turn he made was a dead end. He Tried to run, desperately tried to open locked doors, but there was no escape. No waking from this nightmare. Suddenly a small black shadow began to form beside him. And that small black shadow became a creature. He stared down at a black goat, with white horns. As he watched, the goat gently took Daniel's index finger into its mouth, and bit down.

Daniel awoke with a start. Sweat soaked his skin and pillow as he gasped for breath. He was alone in the bed, Grace was up. What time was it? Not too late, he hoped. It was 9am.

Grace had curled up on the sofa beneath a blanket to read a book. Daniel sat beside her, gave her a kiss on the head.

"You feeling better today?"

She nodded. "Kind of. I couldn't sleep though, been up since six"

"Was it my fault?" Asked Daniel. "I think I

had a rough night."

"Did you? No, it wasn't you. I just thought I heard something, noises downstairs. Probably my imagination but I couldn't get back to sleep so I just got up."

"I wish you'd have woken me. I could have checked."

"You've got enough on your plate. We're both run down and stressed from the move, it'll be fine once we're better."

"Maybe. Sorry for things being so shit."

"Shut up, I told you, it's not your fault." She reached out to stroke his cheek. "More nightmares?"

He shrugged. "They just get weirder and weirder. Does your new mate know anything about what dreams mean?" He grinned halfheartedly. "Because I haven't got a clue!"

"Ellie? I don't know, wouldn't surprise me though. Did you know she does tarot readings too?"

"Oh god, not one of them." He groaned.

"Don't be mean! She's nice."

"Well you haven't even met her yet, how do you know?"

"Alright, I don't… yet, but I've invited her round tomorrow, so we can both find out! Happy?"

The eye roll answered her question sufficiently, but she continued. "I've also got a job interview on Monday."

Daniel perked up. "Really? Where?"

"The cafe in town. Just part time to begin with, but they get really busy in summer, so there will be more hours. I know it's not much, but..."

"What do you mean not much? That's brilliant!"

"I haven't got it yet."

"Rubbish. Why wouldn't you? They'll be begging you to run the place in a week."

"Mmm..." She looked uncertain.

"Listen, why don't you go back to bed for a few hours. Catch up on some sleep then you can be all better for tomorrow."

Grace stared suspiciously at him. "Why, what do you want to do that you'd rather I didn't know about?"

"What's that meant to mean?"

She closed her book and laid it on the coffee table. "I saw the mess in the spare room, and the photos you downloaded onto my laptop."

He opened and closed his mouth like a fish. Searching for where to begin. "Umm... I was going to tell you."

Her expression became a mixture of annoyance and pity, as he continued to dig his hole ever deeper. "I was looking up that graffiti outside and found someone on a forum who knew what it was. That's all.. I was just being nosey."

"And the spare room?"

"Well... you kept hearing those noises..."

"In the ceiling." She added.

"...and I heard something too, so I wondered

if there were mice or something in the old fireplace…"

"Mice. In the fireplace."

"Yes."

"So, are there?"

"I don't know. I haven't finished looking. I didn't want to wake you with the noise."

He glared, daring her to question his motives further, but she knew better than to argue.

CHAPTER 8 - ELLIE

A short, rosy cheeked, middle aged woman with a shock of naturally blonde hair stood in the driveway early next morning, engulfed in a cloud of some kind of musky, floral perfume. Daniel reached the front door first. "You're Ellie I assume?"

"You assume correctly. And you must be Daniel?"

"Dan." He replied defiantly, feeling rather like she was about to ask if his Parents were home.

Grace swatted Daniel to one side and rushed forward to provide Ellie with a warmer welcome and a hug.

"Lovely to meet you, don't mind him." She motioned. "He's in a mood because I wouldn't let him knock a hole in the wall."

Dan rolled his eyes, and gave an emphatic shrug of contempt.

Entirely unphased, Ellie replied. "Ah, well that's men for you! Always wanting to hammer stuff or knock holes in things."

Daniel found himself smirking, as Ellie shot him a sneaky wink. Maybe she wasn't going to be so bad after all.

"Can I get you a coffee or something?" Grace ushered her into the kitchen. "It really is lovely to meet you properly."

"Thank you, why not! What a lovely house. Don't think I've been up this road in years, it hasn't really changed a bit."

Grace handed her a mug and she proceeded to march straight over to the window and nod at the graffiti on the pillar.

"Oops. Someone have an accident with a paint tin?"

Daniel snorted. "Yeh, you could say that. Found it when we moved in."

"Grace was telling me… " She tutted. "I've got some paint remover in the car. In case you need something stronger than soap and water. Do you mind if I get a photo of it first, though? Looks interesting."

"Why is it interesting?" Daniel queried.

"Well it's not your normal sort of Ben woz ere rubbish is it? Seems like someone knows a bit of the old local history."

"You recognise it?" Grace was surprised.

Ellie shrugged, sipping her coffee. "It's not exactly the same, but yes.That circle, with the cross, It's an ancient symbol of the crossroads, you know how a crossroads is steeped in mystery and folklore…"

Grace shook her head and Dan stared blankly at the pair of them.

"They're considered quite special in supernatural terms, there are countless tales of crossroads being used to bury criminals or witches beneath, condemning their spirits to wander the roads for eternity, never finding peace. The fae folk are said to linger at a crossroads hoping to ensnare a passer by, they're also the meeting place for all manner of beings. And then there's the devil." She paused, emphasising the word for effect. " It's a meeting place between worlds you see. A liminal space like the border between earth and sea. Even staircases were feared in the dark ages as witches were said to be able to move between realms using them. Anyhow, this house is well documented for being built on a crossroads back when the village barely existed. They say it used to belong to an old smuggler who had a curse put on him. I'll have to dig out some old books at home, I'm sure I've got the story somewhere."

"It doesn't look that old." Daniel muttered, stiffly.

"Oh this place has certainly been altered over the decades. I'd be willing to bet part of this house has timbers going back centuries."

Grace sighed. "Oh please don't give him any more ideas, he'll be wanting to bring down the ceilings next."

Ellie gave a hearty chuckle and ignored the pained expression that passed between the couple.

"If you want to appease the spirits" She continued. "Just leave out an offering. Bowl of milk or some bread will do."

Daniel couldn't help himself. "You're more likely to appease the local hedgehogs with a feast like that."

Ellie laughed again, seemingly oblivious to the sarcasm, or perhaps choosing to ignore it. "I dare say they might take a fancy too!"

Grace motioned for them to finish up their drinks. "Shall we get going then? I'm really excited to see some of the places you mentioned Ellie. We didn't have anything like this back home. It's all Jack the ripper museums and stuffy old royal country houses."

They piled into Ellie's dilapidated old Land Rover, which smelled of a strange mixture of old grease, and the same floral aroma that Ellie wore, and set off up the hill. They turned onto an even smaller road, that could barely even be considered a road by London standards, more of a farm track. Ellie seemed such an unlikely looking person to be hurtling around in a bulky old 4x4, but strangely it suited her. She chattered on about local landmarks and the families owning much of the land through which they passed. Daniel had to admit, she did know her stuff.

"I never asked what you do for a living Ellie?" He called from the bumpy backseat.

"Oh this and that." She waved. "I run the arts centre in town with a friend, and we put on workshops and talks, that sort of thing. I do a bit part time in the library too. The odd tarot reading, but that's more for fun, ya know?"

He nodded, not really knowing, but more intrigued than he was willing to let on.

Before he could ask anything else, Ellie had swung the car into a small fenced off parking area surrounded by scrubland and curiously stunted, little trees.

"Right then, here we are!"

They jumped out, glad of the coats and wellies they'd been warned to bring, and trudged over the boggy ground to a gravel path.

"This is the abandoned village of Crowan. Gorgeous little place, such a shame it's been left to ruin."

Grace and Daniel followed Ellie down the sloping path into an overgrown wilderness littered with stones and half crumbled cottages. Grace gasped in surprise, "Is that a church?"

Ellie beamed proudly. "It is. You can't go inside any longer, too dangerous, but it used to be beautiful. So simple and understated."

"You wouldn't think anywhere would be left like this in Cornwall? Isn't everything just snapped up and turned into holiday homes?" Daniel said.

"Oh they tried. But the land owners wouldn't have none of it. Would rather see it all fall to bits than have a holiday park on their doorstep."

"Gosh I don't know whether to be sad or pleased!" Said Grace. "Who owns it?"

"Same folks that own the village just up the

way. Not much there either, just a pub and a few cottages. Pretty little woodland though, not many people venture up there, mind you. It's got a bit of a weird vibe. We can pop up and have a look if we have time."

They followed their bubbly guide through the mess of brambles and weeds to a set of steps behind the church. Once at the top, the path seemed to vanish into the sea as a spectacular view spread out before them. They followed the cliff path for a few minutes before it split into two and they were led through a field and into a copse of hawthorn. They picked their way gingerly through, moving slowly so as not to catch their clothes on twigs and prickly things.

Daniel stopped to take a breather and turned back to see the view behind them. The sea had vanished again, but he caught a flicker of movement amongst the trees. He waited to see if someone was following in their footsteps, but no one appeared.

Grace shouted back. "Dan? Hurry up, this is amazing, you have to see it!"

"Coming." He said, taking one last look, certain that he'd seen a figure.

Clambering over loose rock and earth, he reached a clearing beneath the tree cover. It was dark and dingy, late afternoon light in spite of only being about 10am. One tree in particular had been adorned with brightly coloured ribbons. It looked like some strange cross between a maypole and a scarecrow. "Christ on a bike! That's enough to give you nightmares!" He recoiled, only half joking as he manoeuvred around the spikey apparition.

Grace turned to Ellie and mouthed an apology just loud enough to make sure Daniel heard too.

"What? Oh come on..."

"It's a sacred place Dan."

"It's a perfect location for a horror movie, more like. Fine, I'll keep my opinions to myself." He put a hand to his mouth and mimicked a zipper being closed across it.

"Idiot." Grace muttered.

Ellie, who had been silently pretending that she wasn't in the middle of a marital spat, grinned awkwardly. "It's not for everyone. And it's fine Grace, I'm not that easily offended. Come on, let me show you the coolest part..."

They picked their way through the brambles towards a large granite rock. A narrow track had been naively laid with pebbles and stones. The rock had been upended and a hollow chipped out of the centre, to make an altar of sorts. A small carved figure and some well used candles were wedged inside.

Ellie moved to one side of the rock and ushered Grace towards an opening in the ground. Rough stone steps lead down into the darkness.

Grace gasped. "Wow... what's this for? Wait,

you want me to go down there? No way."

Ellie pulled a phone from her pocket and switched on the torch. "It's more atmospheric with candles but this is easier." She laughed. "Follow me."

Daniel stood, arms crossed and a haughty sneer on his face as Grace disappeared into the hole after Ellie. He looked around. The strange wood was really creepy. There wasn't even any bird noises and he could have sworn there was another shadow figure over by the clootie tree. Nope. He was not going to look.

"Dan…" Grace called from the hole. "Come and see this!"

He ventured closer, peering down. He could see lights and movement. Ellie's cheerful face appeared. "Come on, there's just about room for three of us."

He stepped carefully down into the hole in the ground, not at all sure what to expect. He crouched in order to get down the last step and into the curious little cavern.

"Mind your step." Said Grace, grabbing his hand.

A pool of water filled most of the space which appeared to be trickling from the rocks in the wall. Ellie shone the light from her phone around the space. "It's an ancient well. Folk have been coming here to pray or use its holy water to bless the sick for centuries."

For once Daniel was speechless. The glow

from the torch reflected off the glistening walls and it sparkled as though it were alive.

"How deep is that?" He nodded towards the black water at his feet.

"Oh not very. You won't drown if you fall in, you're quite safe."

"Good to know. What's all that stuff over there?"

"Offerings." Ellie replied. "People leave all sorts of things as a thank you to the gods, or the spirits. Mostly just flowers and candles, but sometimes other things."

"That looks like a skull." Daniel peered closer at the natural rock shelves lined with shells, and dried flowers.

Ellie nodded. "Bones too."

Grace shivered. "I don't think I like it down here to be honest. It's got a weird vibe."

"You're in the presence of spirit here. You could leave an offering if you wish, I bet the energy would change pretty quick if you did."

"Oooh I don't know about that. I think I need to get back up top." And with that Grace scurried back up the steps to daylight.

"Is she claustrophobic?" Ellie asked.

"Not usually."

"Ah well. Maybe it's not for her then."

"What d'you mean?"

Ellie paused thoughtfully. "How do you feel down here?"

"Umm... alright I s'pose. It's a bit chilly, but

it's ok."

"Not creepy then?"

"No. I s'pose not. Better than up there with that freaky old tree."

Ellie looked intrigued. "Maybe you should try leaving an offering then. I thought it was Grace they wanted to talk to, but perhaps it's you."

"They?" Daniel gulped.

"The ancient ones, the gods, the spirits, whatever you want to call them. It doesn't really matter to them. They've always been here, in the earth, and us mortals can choose to believe or not, but if we want to, we can tap into the ancient energy and… make use of it."

Daniel wasn't sure whether to bolt back up the stairs and run for home, or go along with this nonsense, but he knew one thing for sure, he felt a sudden surge of nervous energy and anticipation at her words. Ellie held out her hand. "Here, take this." She dropped a small pebble into his palm. "Give it a try." She winked and started to head back up the steps. "You might want to put your torch on though."

By the time he'd fumbled for his phone and got the light working he was completely alone. But it didn't feel awful. He spent a moment just looking around the walls again, then pointed the light into the pool. He dropped the pebble into the water. The ripples faded quicker than he'd anticipated, almost as if the water had absorbed the stone into its very being. It was so black, he realised. That black again. He turned to go up the steps when something caught his eye. A glint of something on the ground. It was a key. It looked old, bulky and made of iron, probably not someone's house key, unless they lived in some posh old 17th Century manor house, but most likely it had been an offering. Either way he knew he should probably leave it there. But something about it made him put the key into his pocket and run back up the steps to the world above.

Grace looked edgy and a little uncomfortable. "Well?"

Daniel shrugged. "I just threw the pebble in the water. Nothing special."

"Nothing?" Ellie inquired with a smile.

"Yeah, nothing." He put his hand into his pocket and found the key there. He swallowed louder than before. "You should have done the same Grace."

"No thanks. I think it's time we headed home anyway, I'm feeling a bit hangry."

On that note, Ellie excitedly offered to buy lunch at the nearby pub. A *welcome to Cornwall* lunch she called it, and it would have been rude to refuse an offer like that. They retraced their footsteps through the wood, the clootie tree not seeming nearly as horrifying to Daniel as it had previously. Once back at the car they only had a few minutes drive up the hill to the tiny village of Trenwyn. Parking on the street outside the pub, they headed inside. It was like stepping back in time. Low ceilings, oak beams and floorboards.

"You could almost imagine this was a smugglers inn," Grace said excitedly.

"It was." Grinned Ellie. "This place is packed with history."

They ordered some sandwiches and a round of drinks, and enjoyed an hour spent listening to more of Ellie's folk tales. Daniel had, to Grace's annoyance, become fascinated by them. For a guy who scoffed at everything 'woo woo' he was suddenly full of questions and seemingly fascinated by Ellie's talents as a Tarot reader.

"Oh that's just something I do for fun really." She brushed off. "I am psychic though, although some people feel more comfortable receiving messages through cards instead of spirits." She leaned forward to whisper, "It all comes from the same place though… just don't tell them that." She giggled to herself as though remembering a specific example of a nervous client.

"So you speak to ghosts?" Daniel asked.

"Well that's putting it bluntly, but yes, you could say that. I don't call them ghosts, it's the energy of a person left behind. The part that doesn't fully move on to the next world, but essentially it's a dead person, yes."

Daniel frowned, opening his mouth to speak then closing it again.

Ellie continued. "I'd be happy to contact someone for you. No charge of course, for a friend."

"What about someone who - "

"Dan!" Grace shot him a warning look and he glared back.

"What if you didn't know if someone were... dead. Could you maybe like, find out. If they were there or not."

"Oh sure. I could feel around. Ask out. Not all the dead want to be called up of course, and you can never be sure you'll get the person you want to talk to, but there's usually some information somewhere. Sounds like you have someone in mind."

Grace interrupted. "I don't think this is a good idea."

"Well what if I do?" Daniel snapped. "Maybe Ellie can actually help figure this situation out, unlike the police!"

Ellie's eyes grew wide. "Police?"

"My Brother. He went missing."

Grace immediately pushed her chair back with an ear splitting screech of wood against the tile flooring. "I think I'd prefer to get home now if you don't mind Ellie. I have some things I need to be getting on with."

"Of course, of course. Not a problem." She bustled merrily.

The journey home was in stark contrast to earlier. They rode in silence most of the way back to Penmerryn. As Ellie dropped them at their door Grace thanked her for the day out and apologised for being a bit short, but Ellie wouldn't hear of it. She gave a nod towards Daniel as they exchanged a look that said, we'll talk again soon.

CHAPTER 9 - CARN MADROW

The ancient monument of Carn Madrow often slips under the radar of most travellers. Its rural and hard to reach location sets it apart from other standing stones. Daniel typed the name into the search engine and was disappointed to see very little in the results. A sparse Wikipedia page and a google map selection which he clicked, and was surprised to discover it wasn't more than a thirty minute drive away. Grace looked over his shoulder as she passed, "What's that?"

"Umm, just some local place, a stone circle or something. Keep hearing about it."

Grace paused, "Looks like a nice place for a picnic doesn't it?"

"Err yeah, that's what I was thinking. Do you fancy it?"

"Why not. Weather's not too bad tomorrow. Could take a brolly just in case. Be nice to get out into the countryside, just the two of us."

Daniel noted the emphasis on *two of us*.

"I'll pop to the shops then, get some supplies."

She nodded. "Don't be too long." They hadn't spoken about the previous day's outing. Daniel assumed she didn't want to remind him that Ellie had essentially offered to help him find his brother. As if he could forget. Things didn't need to be made more tense between them right now, so he kept quiet, but unknown to Grace, he'd nipped back into her messages and found Ellie's email address.

Where was the harm? It was probably all woo woo nonsense but if the police couldn't find Tom, maybe it was time to explore alternative methods.

Once in the car he checked his emails. She'd replied already. Next sunday? His thumbs typed out a hasty "Yes" before his nerve could fail him. The next message popped in almost too quickly, a thumbs up emoji, her phone number and address. He guiltily stuffed the phone into his pocket and started the car.

On his return he found Grace nervously primping herself in the bathroom's full length mirror.

"Do you think I look OK?" She muttered, still smoothing the imaginary wrinkles from her clothes.

"Oh shit, your interview! It's today! You look gorgeous, don't worry."

"Nice save." She grimaced "I dunno... maybe I should have gone with a dress. Trousers might be too corporate."

"Stop worrying. You look amazing, and they will love you whatever you're wearing! What time is it? I'll drive you."

She ummed and ahed some more, turning before the mirror as if the reflection could somehow be altered from a different vantage. "It's not for another couple of hours yet. Hmm, I don't know…"

"OK, come downstairs. You are as ready as you're ever going to be and we're gonna have a celebratory drink."

"I haven't got the job yet!" She exclaimed.

"No, but you will! And you clearly need some dutch courage. Come on woman, get your arse downstairs."

"Don't you dare try and get me drunk Mr Gibson!"

"Would I?" he smirked innocently.

Three hours later Grace hopped back into the passenger seat of the car and let out a joyous yell.

"Does that mean it went well?" Daniel asked eagerly.

"I got it!" Grace squealed. "They said yes on the spot!"

He leaned over and hugged her. "Told you. You're amazing. Well done!"

"Thank you. Whew… that was so nerve wracking. How stupid of me. It's only a job in a cafe, and I don't even start yet. The lady I'm replacing doesn't leave until the end of the month."

"Well it's been a while since you had to go for an interview, and it's a new place, new job. It's fine. Don't worry. You got it, that's the main thing. And it looks like a nice place!" He tilted his head to look through the windscreen approvingly at the sprawling whitewashed building before them. Originally a large pub/restaurant that had added a separate tea room for light refreshments. "It's a bit more than just a cafe!"

Grace shrugged. "Yeh, well they only want someone for the tea room part time at the moment, but I might get more work in the main restaurant in the spring, when the holiday season starts."

Dan smiled at her. "Well I'm proud of you anyway. And those lot back in London would kill for a job in Cornwall, whatever it was, coz when they're stuck in an office in the summer heat, we'll be here eating cream teas and heading to the beach for an evening swim!

The next morning the sun rose amid a haze of swirling grey clouds. The weather report hadn't sounded too promising either, but Dan could hear Grace singing in the bathroom as she readied herself, still basking in the glow of yesterday's good news. A shadow of guilt washed over him, like a vast black rain cloud blocking out the sun on a hot day, but he didn't know why.

"You ready?" She called, bouncing happily down the stairs.

"Yep. All set." Daniel nodded, a forced grin frozen in place.

"What's up?"

"Nothing. Why?"

Grace peered suspiciously at him. "If you don't want to go we can put it off until the weather's better."

"Nah… it'll be fine." He waved her away, slightly annoyed that she could always spot a fake smile from a mile away, and yet, he'd tried it anyway.

They threw the bags into the back seat along with coats and umbrellas for the worst case scenario, and set off for the moors. A beautiful, rugged, lonely stretch of scrubland coming eventually to an abrupt halt where the edge of the land met jagged shards of rock and treacherously high cliffs straight down to the sea.

Pulling out of the drive they passed by a group of teenagers laughing and pushing each other into the road. Dan grumbled and beeped the horn at them, but he received only cheers and whoops of laughter in return. "Stupid kids!"

"They're only messing about Dan. Having fun. You remember, that thing we used to have… F U N." She spelled it slowly for him.

"You didn't think it was funny when they

were having F U N in our garden the other week."

Grace gave a snort of indignance and folded her arms. The universal signal for 'this conversation is done'.

They drove the rest of the way in silence. Grace stepped out onto the grass verge where they had parked and glanced up and down the tiny road. "It looks like we'll be ok here. Didn't realise there wasn't a proper carpark."

"I suppose it's not popular enough to have a carpark. It's not even close to a village for dog walking."

"Which way is it? Not through that overgrown field I hope." Grace pointed, her face fell at the sea of weeds and nettles blowing in the harsh wind.

Dan was busy heaving his rucksack onto his back. "I think there's a path down the side, look!"

It was more of a rough track than a path, but it was labelled with a wooden stake and small public footpath sign, so they followed it. The track, they realised, had only served to provide false hope. It dwindled, growing narrower and more overgrown with each bend they rounded. It was muddy too. Sticky and slippery. They hopped over puddles of varying sizes, glad of their brand new hiking boots but wishing they'd picked an easier walk with which to break them in.

Half an hour later and they were still wading through a tangle of unruly nettles and tall grasses. Conversation was limited as the terrain was uphill and had revealed just how out of shape they truly were. Dan's headache had returned and his temples throbbed with every step as he scowled at the weeds seemingly determined to thwart his stride.

"For Christ's sake." He muttered. "How much further is this damned place?"

Grace shrugged unhelpfully. Choosing not to engage.

"Well I'm all for turning back and going for a takeaway. No old bits of rock can be worth all this hassle. No wonder it's not busy!"

Grace was about to speak when she glimpsed something ahead. "Hey, I think we've made it."

The tall, stone pillar loomed high above the wild grass like an eldritch sentinel. They stopped in their tracks. It almost felt like they were being watched, and they could do nothing but stare back.

Grace shuddered beneath its gaze. "Come on. Let's see what the fuss is all about then."

Daniel followed her out of the weeds onto the moorland and as they grew closer they could see that five smaller stones encircled the tall one, their faded pockmarked scars suggesting that they had been here a very long time.

Daniel walked up to the nearest stone and reached out a hand to touch its weatherbeaten surface. Despite its rough appearance the surface was smooth like marble and cold to the touch. Rain water had collected in tiny pockets like rock pools on the beach. He half expected to find a small webbed creature hiding there beneath some seaweed. He pulled his hand away and looked up again at the central pillar. It was less like a pillar from this new vantage point, and more like something trapped within the stone itself. Something monstrous and wild. Something that had once struggled to free itself, and might once more try given the opportunity.

Grace found a dry patch on the crest of a small hill, beside some boulders, and shook out the blanket. She sat down, knees drawn up, and poured from the flask. "Coffee?" She called.

"Hell yes. It's cold now that we've stopped walking." He took the hot cup in both hands and sipped. His headache eased slightly with the welcome heat.

"So, did you find any information on this place?" Grace inquired.

"Not much really. Should have asked Ellie, I bet she knows more."

Grace's eyebrow twitched. "Mmmm."

"What's up? You gone off her now you've actually met in person?"

"No."

"I quite like her."

"So do I!" Grace replied indignantly.

Daniel sat down beside her and rummaged

in the bag for a sausage roll. "So what is it then?"

She side eyed him. "You know what."

"You mean the seance thing."

"Well obviously I mean the seance thing! It just sounds like a really bad idea."

She snatched a sausage roll from the pack he held out and chewed it vigorously.

"Don't be annoyed Grace. She means well. And to be honest I think it might be worth investigating, hold on, let me finish… I need some sort of closure of this. The police can't help and I know this is a bit weird but what if it works? What if she can at least tell me if he's… ya know. Gone."

Grace was quiet for a moment. "And what if she tells you that? Will you believe her? Will you stop looking?"

He looked downwards and aimlessly picked crumbs from his jacket. "Yes. Maybe. I want to give it a try, Grace."

She stared out at the stone circle, her face a mask that he couldn't read. "OK." She whispered softly.

Daniel stared in astonishment. "Really?" He hadn't expected her to agree, although he had fully intended to go ahead with it.

She gave him a brief glance. "I want you to remember this conversation though."

"I will. I promise I will."

The heavy scent of damp earth reminded them of where they sat, and Grace pulled her collar up a little. It wasn't really cold and the wind had now dropped to an eerie stillness that stifled all sound of the natural world, as though a volume control had been turned right down.

A few gaps appeared in the sodden grey sky above, revealing tiny patches of iridescent blue and a beam of sunlight sliced through the clouds like a laser beam, to highlight perfectly the clearing in which they sat.

"Isn't that beautiful?" Gasped Grace. "It makes this place look so different suddenly. Special."

Daniel couldn't help but agree with her, but as he watched the golden beam weaken and fade with each gathering cloud his stomach churned and something inside him tightened. He hunched over his rapidly cooling coffee and tried to look like he was fine, but he could see Grace eying him again.

"Got a bit of indigestion." he muttered, rubbing his chest. "Probably the sausage roll."

Grace still looked concerned.

"Think the sun's coming back out." He nodded upwards, as the clouds parted, hoping to distract her attention. "Might be a nice day after all."

With the return of the sunlight came a chattering of birdsong, and a sweet scent wafting intermittently from some species of wildflower nearby. Grace stretched out like a cat, lying back, closing her eyes to bask in the small, distant warmth that only a winter sun can provide.

Daniel stood up, writhed a bit, then stretched his arms out to relieve his stiff muscles from lugging the heavy bag all the way up here and muttered something about having a wander. He'd begun to feel giddy, slightly nauseous and prayed fervently that it really was only indigestion as he took a few unsteady steps towards the circle of stones. He reached for one, a large boulder that he could lean on for a moment. Taking a few deep breaths he was relieved to find the nausea passing. He continued his exploration of the outer ring of stones noting his desire to touch each one as he went. Each stone, he realised, felt different. Some smooth and cold, others warmer, with a roughness or a sharp bite. Eventually he returned to where he had begun and knowing that he had no choice but to approach the one he'd been assiduously avoiding. The sentinel stone.

Daniel's pulse began to race and his legs not fully recovered began to tremble once more, his reaction was so visceral and so excessive he almost laughed, but something deep within his bones told him that this was no laughing matter. Something in his DNA screamed a warning. Run.

Though he did not run. He put one foot in front of the other until he was mere inches from the peculiarly pitted, splayed edges of this lump of granite. It's just a piece of rock, he told himself over and over as he reached out a hand, as he had done with the smaller surrounding stones. His fingertips grazed the trunk of this monstrosity and he felt… nothing. The strange energy flatlined as he held the palm of his hand against solid stone. Nothing. As though he had pulled the plug by anchoring himself to the source, all his uneasiness, all the unpleasant physical symptoms just vanished. His jaw fell open with surprise as he craned his head to look up. It was at least three times his height, and perhaps twice his width, but more importantly, it no longer felt alive.

Grace called from the blanket. "You alright over there?"

He turned his head to meet her gaze and offered her a schoolboy grin. "Of course!"

"So you're feeling better now?"

"Much better. I'm a bit hungry though."

Grace chuckled. "Well I wouldn't risk another sausage roll if I were you. Shall we see if we can find a cafe somewhere?"

"Are you bored already? We just got here." Daniel exclaimed.

Grace checked her phone. "We've been here nearly two hours. I had a nice little snooze while you were worshipping your new god." She laughed, pushing herself to her feet. "My arse has gone to sleep. Ouch!" She smacked at her backside as if to wake it.

Daniel frowned. "Two hours?" He checked his own phone as if he would catch her in a lie. "I don't get it…"

"Come on, we've still got that massive trek back to the car yet. I'll drive. Not sure you're very with it today."

Daniel couldn't deny that it would probably be safer if she took the wheel. Still in a daze he helped her pack up the blanket and heaved the bag over his shoulder.

They decided on an early pub dinner at The Wreckers back in Penmerryn. They pulled into a side road on the quay and walked the short distance to the pub. The sun was still out, if a little hazy, and glimmers of light caught the tips of the waves out at sea. The air was fresh and salty and it felt good to be buffeted by a breeze again after the stale breath of the stagnant moorland valley.

They seated themselves by the window, in the area reserved for dining. Dan cautiously eyed the room hoping that the creepy Mr Blackthorn wasn't hanging around. He didn't fancy another encounter, especially not with Grace in tow. Luckily there was no sign of the goblinesque little man, only a handful of regulars and a dog lying patiently beneath a table awaiting his treasured contraband.

They ordered their food and sat back to wait with a cold lager. Grace seemed preoccupied with typing a particularly long message to someone on her phone and Daniel peered across the table at it.

"Oy, nosy!" she grinned. "It's just someone I met in town, when I went for my job interview."

"Oh?" Daniel muttered, feigning disinterest.

"They're involved with that Winter lights festival I told you about… "

"Festival?"

"I told you… " She huffed, pausing her rapid typing to move her drink aside for the plates of food that had arrived. "It's a thing that happens in the village every year for the solstice. A procession of lanterns and people dressed up. It's meant to protect the village from the darkness of winter and demons and all that, and welcome back the light of a new year."

"Sounds lovely!" He deadpanned.

"Oh stop it. Why do you always have to be so sarcastic?"

He shrugged but Grace had already gone back to her typing.

He picked at his salad. Why did he always make fun of things? He knew why. It was easier to poke fun than to accept there were forces in this world that he could not understand, or control, and given all that had happened recently, it was becoming harder to keep up the pretence. He pondered the last time he'd sat in this pub and the things that crazy little man had said. And the map to Carn Madrow. What was it about those stones? He shook it off. Better to bury those thoughts alongside everything else if he was to ever feel anything even resembling normality again.

CHAPTER 10 - TOM

The rest of the week came and went, largely unnoticed. The ever present grey cloud and equally grey sea mirrored Dan's emotions as he sat by the bedroom window waiting for a knock at the door. He knew Grace was apprehensive about seeing Ellie again, and even more so of the reason she was coming over this afternoon, but this was something he needed to do. In order to move forward with his life, one way or another. He was stagnating, and he knew it. Going through the motions of life without ever really experiencing it. Even when he wasn't thinking about Tom, which to be fair was not much of the time, he just couldn't find that spark within himself to fully engage with the world. Or his wife. And now she was spending half her time texting some new friends she'd met, supposedly about the plans for this Winter Festival, but Dan wondered. Was that all it was about? He'd heard the name Steve once or twice, and she'd taken the last phone call outside in the garden. The incessant brooding had brought on a new headache, he closed his eyes against the glare of daylight and jumped as the doorbell shrieked, jolting him back into the present.

He jogged down the stairs, casting an eye into rooms as he passed, searching for Grace. She was in the lounge, flicking aimlessly through the tv channels.

He flung open the front door. "Hi, come in."

Ellie beamed. "Thank you. I'm glad you and Grace changed your minds."

He pulled a face to indicate that it wasn't a total conversion on Grace's part, Ellie accepted the warning with a silently mouthed "Ah."

"Grace, Ellie's here!" He called, waving his guest through into the lounge.

The women's greeting was far more subdued than their previous one, but Ellie smiled no less warmly. She understood that people new to this were hesitant and sceptical, and often so far out of their comfort zone that it was almost an unthinkable sort of magic. When the reality is that using a sixth sense is entirely natural. In all walks of life it's an ingrained piece of the puzzle, for both humans and animals. Some call it a survival instinct; that which makes a person suddenly turn their car in a different direction only to discover that an accident had occurred just moments later. Or that sense of knowing a family member was in need of a phone call. Of course, the psychic abilities that allowed a person to use mediumship, or read tarot cards is a little bit more intense than that, and as Ellie began to explain, it had run in her family for generations.

Ellie cleared a space on the coffee table, setting out a candle and a pack of tarot cards that she'd chosen specifically for today's session. She admitted that she didn't always use them, but they can be helpful if need be.

"Can I get you anything? Do you want a drink first or..." Grace stammered, switching off the tv, perhaps a little too keen to delay the proceedings.

Ellie shook her head. "I'm fine. I'll just take a moment to clear my head and then we can start. I don't need any bells and whistles to make a connection." She knelt easily on the floor, setting her hands on the table on either side of the candle and took a series of slow, deep breaths.

Dan perched restlessly on the armchair, his leg juddering annoyingly as if he had a nervous tick. Grace swatted at him. Equally as nervous but just better at hiding it.

Ellie opened her eyes and looked directly at Dan. "You have questions regarding your Brother." It was a statement rather than a question, but he nodded and started to speak. She held up her hand to shush him. "I can sense a group of men with you. They feel like family, your Uncle perhaps. Has your father passed over as well?"

He looked dumbfounded, but nodded.

"Mmmm... was he a tall man, slim build.

Bearded. Dark hair?"

"Yes, that's him!"

"He is showing me a blue door, with roses growing by it."

"That's our old house, where I grew up. Yes. Yes!" Dan turned his head to Grace, his eyes shone with excitement. Grace looked on, unsmiling. Her gaze flickering between them.

Ellie frowned, "I don't see your Uncle or your Brother." She stated.

"But you said the men were family." Daniel fidgeted some more.

"Yes, they feel like relatives, but ancestral. Your father's line going back many centuries."

"So where's Uncle John?" He asked.

"Where is John?" Ellie repeated, concentrating so deeply the lines in her forehead creased to a heavy frown. "It's very strange, your father is showing me something, but I can't make it out properly. It's like a black hole. Something he holds in his hands, like a box. It seems invisible to me... I can't get a sharp focus on it."

Now it was Dan's turn to frown. "What does that mean? Does he know where Tom is?"

"I'm asking." Ellie muttered, closing her eyes. "He is not there, not on the other side, but he is not here either. I don't understand. What do I need to know spirit? He is nearby, but trapped. Unable to move forward or back." She reopened her eyes and slumped to sit on the floor as she appeared to lose the connection.

Grace sat rigidly in her chair. "Are you alright?" She asked.

Ellie nodded. "It's very odd. Something is definitely amiss here, with Tom's disappearance. The police found nothing, you say?"

Dan shook his head. "They reckoned he was dead or didn't want to be found. But, you don't think he's dead? Is that what you're saying?"

"He is not where the dead reside, but I can't find him among the living either." Her signature smile had long since faded and she attempted to coax it back, somewhat unsuccessfully. "I'll try the tarot, and see what information comes. They can be more useful to work with concerning matters of the physical world."

She opened the pack of Rider Waite cards, holding them lightly in the palms of her hands while she whispered something over them, a blessing, she said, as she shuffled the decorative cards and laid a spread out on the table before them. Daniel held his breath. The tension within him was strung tight as a bow and he nervously avoided looking into the corners of the room in case the shadows he could see there were more than just shadows.

"A moment please." Ellie sighed. "This is telling me as much as I have already received. The answer to the question is between worlds. Not dead, not living, but close."

Daniel leaped on her words as a dog would a fresh meaty bone. "You're saying he's not dead!

You're definitely saying that. And that he's nearby. So that can only mean he's ill, or unconscious maybe?" He jumped up from his uncomfortable perch. "We need to check the hospital again, or - "

"Wait." Ellie's voice cut sharply through his elation. "While that is possible, I don't sense that he is ill or harmed in any way. Now I'm not always right or course but - "

"I don't care, that HAS to be it! What other explanation could there be?"

"Dan. I don't like to give people unpleasant news, or say things that might scare them, but I feel very strongly that I should give you a warning."

"About what?"

"I'd advise you to stop searching for your Brother. Whatever this means, I believe that finding him will not bring the peace you seek. In fact, I'd go as far as to say you should not stay here in this house, or even in Cornwall."

Grace gasped in horror. "What a horrible thing to say Ellie!"

"I'm sorry, I know it is, but I do mean it. For your own safety you should leave." She implored.

Dan collapsed back into the armchair, lost for words. He shook his head. "No.. no!" He studied Ellie's face, she seemed rattled. "What are you not saying?" He flung back at her.

She stared back, like a rabbit caught in headlights. "I'm not sure.. I..." Her words faltered and died on her lips. "I truly did not ever expect to say this to anyone. And in all the years I've been reading for people I've never had to. I'm not even sure that I believe it."

Grace got abruptly to her feet, wavering as she did so. "Just say it Ellie. Please. Spit it out."

"Truthfully? I sense something malevolent attached to this. A dangerous energy. There is a person, or... something... that wishes you harm. Your family is being stalked by something evil." Her voice cracked as it wavered. "There. Is that blunt enough?"

Grace's hand had flown to cover her mouth and they all now stood circling the table in complete shocked silence. "This is madness. I knew this would be a terrible idea Dan, I warned you to let this go." She sobbed.

"I agree, it is mad, but don't you see Grace, this is GOOD news! Tom is nearby, I must be able to find him. Ellie, can you get any more on his location? Is that a thing you could do?"

She nodded. "I can try, but... you want me to carry on?"

"Yes I want you to carry on. If he's injured or trapped somewhere we need to get help!" He shouted.

Ellie's hands trembled as she shuffled the cards once more, kneeling again before the table. She cautiously turned the cards over and laid each one precisely with an audible 'flick'. The candle guttered and hissed for a moment as a lump of wax melted into the flame.

"There is a house. Maybe a farmhouse? Somewhere lonely. Maybe you've been there before, perhaps you know it. It feels familiar. It feels like this house, but it can't be this one."

"He's trapped here? In this house?" Dan couldn't help but interrupt.

"Yes, and no… I mean, it's somewhere connected to here. I'm sorry Dan, that's really all I can give you. I'm sorry." She backed away, shoving her belongings back into her bag as she did so. Turning to Grace she said, "I meant what I said about leaving. This place will not bring you the peace you seek. I'm so sorry Grace, this is not what I expected at all."

Grace's stern, cold features gave all the response she needed as Ellie hurriedly excused herself, slipping quietly from the room and closing the front door softly behind her.

"Great! Thanks Grace, now you've upset her!"

"Me? You are joking?" She spluttered as Dan raced outside.

"Ellie, wait… please, hold on." He called.

She paused, holding the car door ajar. "Dan, I really can't help you any more." She apologised.

"No, but hold on, I wanted to ask you…" He pushed the door closed, preventing her from getting in. "Back at that strange well, what did you mean then, when you said you thought the spirits wanted to talk to Grace but maybe it was me after all? Why did you think it was Grace?"

Ellie frowned, trying to recall that conversation. "Oh, I just had a feeling I was supposed to take her there, or both of you. I mean, I only presumed it was Grace because she seemed so much more receptive than you. I should have guessed really. They wanted to show you there is more out there, things beyond our understanding."

"Ellie, I lied to you about something. When I went down to the pool and left the offering, I said nothing happened, but it did."

She raised her eyebrows. "Tell me.."

"I saw something on the ground as I was about to leave, and I picked it up. I mean, I know I shouldn't have taken it, it could have been an offering someone else had left. Maybe they think I stole it, the spirits or gods or whatever they are."

Ellie's voice was calm, but she bristled with apprehension. "What did you find?"

Dan reached into his back pocket and pulled out the rusty old key. "This. I don't know what made me pick it up in the first place. It just seemed like what I was supposed to do. Was that wrong?" He tried to hand it to Ellie but she recoiled.

"If you felt it was for you, then it was. I have no place touching it. I wonder if they were already speaking to you, answering the questions you've asked me today. They gave you a key Daniel. Now I suppose you must find the lock it belongs to."

"A lock?" He racked his brain for the answer. "I know you've done all you can. And thank you!

I mean it, thank you! But tell me if there is something else that I can do, anything!"

Ellie caught sight of the graffiti on the gate post and winced, as if she'd forgotten it was ever there. Dan followed her gaze. "You think that's got something to do with this?"

"I… don't know. Maybe." She glanced uneasily at the paint again. "Is that what connects the house perhaps? Like a way marker…."

Dan slapped his own forehead. "Oh my god, yes. I did some research online and found an old forum where someone posted an image of something like it, asking for help. They were being targeted or something. I thought it was some weird shit the local kids were into, but…"

"I don't think this is down to the local kids, Dan. I think you need to let this go and move far away from here to be honest. Maybe you should return the key to the well and see if things quieten down. I'll ask a friend to help me clear the energy around you." She tilted her head at the graffiti. "And get that removed if you can. Every trace of it. Look after yourself Daniel. You and Grace."

She slid hastily into the driver's seat and drove away from the house. Daniel stared at the tracks her wheels had made in the gravel until his eyes blurred. His head swam with the knowledge that his Brother might still be alive, and knew that he'd do anything to track him down.

CHAPTER 11 - THE ORDER OF DECAY

"Are you going to ignore me all day?" Asked Grace, lunch time the next day. "We should talk about what happened."

"I'm not ignoring you, and no. I don't need to talk about it. You were right, she's crazy and I should never have trusted her."

Grace kept her silence, knowing no good would come of pressuring him into a discussion, but her belly churned as she recalled Ellie's words. It had all sounded completely crazy of course, but Ellie had been so certain and the expression on her face had revealed a great deal about her sincerity.

Daniel continued on. "I promised you that I would let things go afterwards, no matter what, and that's what I'm doing. If she thinks we're giving up this house and running back to London based on a tarot reading from some crazy woman we hardly know, she can think again."

"OK then. So what's the plan?"

"Plan?" He squinted curiously at her.

"For today. For the month, the rest of our

lives? What happens next?"

"Well for starters we finish decorating this damned house and make it a home." He muttered, angrily scuffing at a patch of flaking paint on the skirting. He shot a dark look out of the window. "Beginning with that."

Much of the afternoon was taken up with Daniel's strenuous efforts to restore the granite gate post to its former glory. Luckily the paint had already begun to flake and fade, so a good scrub with a chemical paint remover, courtesy of Ellie, completed the task and with the graffiti gone, so was a major source of tension, he realised. He called Grace out to admire his work, beaming with pride. "Check it out. Good as new!"

She gave an approving smile in return. "Nice work! And while you've been doing that I got dinner in the slow cooker and started stripping the wallpaper in the spare room."

Daniel raised his eyebrows. "Oh?"

"Well I figured we should freshen that room up too. I mean, it's a good guest bedroom or even, well… maybe a kids room one day. I mean, when we're ready to try again."

"That sounds like a plan!" He smiled, stepping forward to kiss her forehead affectionately. "Let's get something to eat and I'll come and give you a hand."

"What's the rush? We can carry on tomorrow."

"Strike while the iron's hot and all that! Besides, I need to get this done. Need to move on."

"OK, but I've got a rehearsal up at the school tomorrow evening. Remember?"

Grace sighed at the blank stare he gave her. "The festival preparations! I've told you a hundred times. You could come along too, you might enjoy a change of scenery. It would get you out of the house!"

He glowered at nothing in particular, deep in thought, then shook his head. "No. I don't think so. That's not my kind of thing."

Grace strolled back to the house, calling over her shoulder. "You might be surprised, you might actually like it! And it would be good for you to meet some people."

He scooped up the bucket and brushes muttering beneath his breath. "Like you I suppose. Anyone in particular I should meet, Grace? Someone named Steve maybe?" He followed her into the house as that old familiar black mood settled over him again like a swarm of invisible flies. He dumped the cleaning supplies in the hallway and went to wash his hands in the upstairs bathroom. A sudden sharp pain pierced his temples and he gripped the basin with both hands, breathing heavily. Grace's voice floated up the stairs to tell him dinner was on the table. Something about it irritated him. He swallowed the feeling down and called back, "OK."

Dinner was eaten in relative silence. Daniel brooding over who knows what, and Grace still focused on her winter festival preparations. She was used to his moodiness, she'd seen enough of it back in London, and although it had begun to fade prior to the move, those dark silences had returned with a vengeance and were now almost a daily occurrence.

They finished up in the kitchen and decamped to the spare room where Grace had already emptied it of bedding and junk, and covered the furniture in dust sheets. She had started on the fireplace wall. It already had a big hole in it, she'd figured, so why not? Grace caught Daniel gazing a little sheepishly at the secret excavation site. "You can knock out the fireplace tomorrow if you want?"

He nodded. Still wary of being pulled into conversation. It felt like a trick somehow and he waited for the questions to begin again. She pretended that she couldn't see his guardedness and chattered on."We can put everything behind us now. Fresh start." Though as she spoke, she averted her eyes not wanting to spark any more battles, and tired of walking on eggshells all the time . A home and a happy family wasn't that much to ask, was it?

They made short work of the paper stripping, and when three black bin liners sat in the corner, brimming with torn and faded 1980's grey and pink wallpaper, they stood back to admire the mess. The plaster wasn't in bad condition and once a few holes had been filled and perhaps a bit of anti-mold paint around the window, it would be ready for something new. Grace was already talking about a trip to the DIY shop, but something caught Dan's eye and her voice became a dull drone in the background. He bent to get a closer look. In one corner, at the base of the wall where it met the skirting board was a small brownish stain. It looked like an old water stain where perhaps there had been a leak. He knelt down and poked at it. The plaster crumbled a little, came away beneath his finger like sand. A gap revealed itself between the crumbly patch of wall and the old wooden skirting board, it was big enough to get his thumb into, and then suddenly more of the wall began to disintegrate. A vast hole appeared in what had moments ago seemed to be solid plaster, and now fell to dust on the old pale blue carpet.

Grace stopped mid sentence and gasped in horror as Dan moved his hand gingerly up the wall until he found a firm place once more.

"Most of it's rotten." he growled, picking now at the skirting below which also appeared to be on its last legs. He held up a few splinters of wood to demonstrate.

"But how?" Grace stammered.

"Dry rot probably." Daniel huffed in disappointment. "So much for thinking we could just paint a few walls."

Grace slumped on to the bed. "But we can't afford to start getting builders in. Do you think it's just in here?"

Dan shrugged. "No idea until we check. That stuff can spread all over the place." He angrily banged free some more of the plaster and peered inside the wall. There's a few wooden struts got it too. That or wood worm. Fantastic." He said with just a hint of sarcasm.

Grace pointed to the area in the corner by the stain, just inside the newly revealed cavity. "What is that?" She asked pointedly, with a tone of disgust.

The small dead creature lay curled into itself, and shrivelled like dried leaves.

"Ugh! That's horrible." She gasped, hurriedly unwrapping a black bin bag from the roll. She held it open whilst turning her head away, eyes closed, as if merely breathing the musty scent of death wasn't bad enough.

Daniel scooped it out with two wallpaper scrapers and attempted to heave it into the bag. A bit of it fell off onto the carpet and Grace squealed loudly. "Oh god.. Ewwww, pick it up! what is it anyway?"

"Hold the bag still then." He muttered. "I don't know, it could be a huge rat I suppose."

Grace risked a wary glance at the near desiccated animal. "Ewwww. How would a rat get inside a wall?"

"Can't see any holes for it to crawl through. Maybe someone walled it in by accident... or not." Daniel felt his gorge rise as he picked up the fallen bits in his hand and threw them into the bag.

"That's disgusting. Why would someone leave a dead rat inside the wall?"

"I wouldn't be so sure it was already dead." Daniel replied slowly. He could see marks on the wooden strut it had been curled next to, and the mysterious stains continued along the floor inside the cavity. His gaze went to the fireplace wall, and the exploratory holes he'd knocked into it just recently.

Grace followed his gaze. "You don't think..."

"I don't know. The plaster is new there, but maybe John was just repairing it."

Dan went to the shed for some heavy duty tools and soon there was a much larger hole. He stared into the rubble.

"Shit!"

Grace peered anxiously round the door. She'd been lingering in the bathroom, pretending to sort washing. "What?" Her mouth gaped and she mouthed a silent "OH!" As Daniel stepped back from the opening. A smell rose from the entangled mess that filled the dusty hearth. The smell of age, and earth, and decaying matter. A parcel of bones encased in leathery feline flesh, not yet entirely dry. A sob rose in Grace's throat. "How could he? What kind of a man was he to treat animals this way?" She stared accusingly at Dan, as if he could somehow have known this about his Uncle and not told her.

Dan stared, unflinching, at the gruesome image. The collection of tiny corpses had seemingly been placed there inside a blanket or a bag of some sort. The fabric now shredded and stained, lay in rags. Forming a macabre sort of nest for its grisly inhabitants. "Maybe he had it in for cats." Daniel said, stupidly and yet not fully believing what his eyes told him.

"He was fucking monster!" Grace raged. Tears making tracks in the dust on her cheeks.

"Go downstairs." Said Dan quietly. "I'll get this cleared out."

"But…"

"Grace. Please."

"You said you heard noises." Grace whispered.

"They've been dead a while. Longer than Uncle John has."

"Dan, what are we going to do about all of … this?" She stared forlornly at the wrecked and rotten walls of her home.

"We'll get someone in to look at it after Christmas. I doubt anyone would be available until then anyway. I'm sure it won't be as bad as you think."

Daniel ventured back to the old shed at the side of the house and peered into the gloom, searching for something useful amongst all the rubbish. He grabbed his new spade and saw some old sacking on the shelf. He dragged it out before realising too late, that it looked fairly similar to the wrecked fabric upstairs in that hole. With the dead creatures.

He pulled on some gardening gloves and strode back inside the house. Digging the mess out of the small tomb was easier than he'd expected. The fragile bodies had fused together where they'd touched. Lying against and on top of one another in their final futile attempts to find freedom. He counted five that he could make out. Their nightmarish little faces frozen into ghoulish masks that seemed so unreal.

Once the unpleasant job was done, Dan carried all the bags of rubbish and wallpaper out with them and pushed them down as deep into the bin as they would go. Then he went back upstairs and opened the wardrobe door, where he'd stored his brother's belongings just a few weeks ago. He began to question once more why Tom had been here. And how well did Tom know Uncle John? So many secrets. So many skeletons in closets, and now even in the very walls themselves. Fueled by anger and disgust, he pulled Tom's belongings from the shelf, hesitating only at the rucksack. His old school bag, that had reawakened so many fond memories, now tarnished. Ruined with the taint of something so very wrong. In a daze he carried those too outside to the bin and hurled them in amongst the remains.

"What are you doing?" Asked Grace.

"Getting rid of something I don't want anymore. That's all."

"You don't mean that, you don't know that Tom was involved in this!"

"No, I don't, but maybe it's time I accepted he's not the person I thought he was."

"Does that mean you've changed your mind about looking for him?" She asked.

He paused to think for a moment. "No."

CHAPTER 12 - WINTERTIDE

Grace stood by the open back door, breathing the chill winter air. The scent of old rain hung heavy, soaking into the soft earth. Lying in quiet pools on the leaves, and of the rain yet to come, gathering ominously in the clouds above.

She closed the door with a thunk, pulled on her boots and checked her phone. Still no response from Dan. He'd supposedly only gone out to get some new paint brushes and cleaner but she suspected his disappearing act was mainly to avoid being badgered into coming with her this afternoon, or worse still, that she wouldn't be able to go either. He'd made no secret of the fact that he was jealous of the interest she'd shown in this project. She blew out her cheeks with an exasperated sigh. If only he'd make an effort to find new friends himself, but then on the other hand, perhaps it would be better if he didn't come. The way his moods were lately he'd likely end up insulting or offending half the village and she was so looking forward to this festival. Helping out with the preparations she felt like she was part of something special for once, and the kids from the local school who she'd been helping to make lanterns with, were some of the loveliest children she could imagine. No, it was definitely better if Daniel wasn't involved, she decided. For everyone's sake.

A white taxi with CC Cabs emblazoned along the side, pulled up in the driveway and she picked up her bag. He'd pretend to be racked with guilt at not having the car back in time for her to leave, but no way was he going to spoil her fun. She climbed into the back seat and sent him another brief text. "No rush, I got a taxi. See u later x" Her phone beeped almost instantly and she smiled knowingly, but it wasn't from Dan.

"Hi, just wondered if you're coming this afternoon?I'd hoped to see you there. Steve."

She smiled as she read it through and her thumbs quickly replied. "I'm on my way!"

Daniel arrived half an hour later. He swerved into the driveway and raced for the front door in a flap, gasping for breath as though he'd run a mile. "Grace, I'm sorry! Shit, you won't believe the traffic… I'll drop you off… you aren't that late are you?" The silence was so loud his voice seemed to echo around him sounding as hollow as his apology. "Shit!" he said again. He wandered into the kitchen to see if she'd left a note, then almost as an afterthought he pulled his phone from his back pocket. "Shitting shit!" he muttered.

He typed quickly, "Just missed you! So sorry. What time do you want picking up? Xxx" He pressed send and hovered over the text, waiting for a reply that didn't come. He typed another message and stared hopefully at it like a naughty dog begging for a treat he didn't deserve. Disappointed, he threw his phone down on the kitchen worktop and reached into the fridge for a bottle of lager. Fine, he muttered to himself, if you're off gallivanting about, I can enjoy the peace and quiet by myself! His phone suddenly began to ring, the vibration echoed through the countertop. He snatched it up only to see the caller was his Mum. He hesitated too long and she rang off. The phone gave another beep and a message popped up on the screen.

"What's all this about dead animals in the house? And why did I have to hear it from Grace? She's worried enough about you. Call me."

He grumbled through a mouthful of cold lager. Why couldn't Grace just keep her mouth shut? No one else had needed to know anything for fucks sake. He slammed the glass bottle down on the counter top with such force that some of its contents overspilled in a spreading pool of froth. Damnit!

A flame ignited deep within his chest. That familiar sensation like heartburn crept slowly through his veins. An insidious crawling inside his chest that seemed to set fire to his lungs and his heart only this time it took hold of his throat as well. Breath caught in his throat as if a hand physically gripped him. Unseen fingers closed around his windpipe, blocking his air. He froze. Was this some kind of panic attack? He gasped and sucked in a lungful of oxygen and the sensation vanished as quickly as it had arrived.

Staggering forward, he slammed his hand down onto the countertop to steady himself but it slipped in the spilt lager. Unable to catch himself he fell to the floor, landing hard on the base of his spine. He lay there a moment, stunned. What is happening to me? His vision blurred and he crawled to standing again only now, the fear gave way to anger, like a damn bursting. A vast irrational rage engulfed him like a tidal wave, boiling and surging as it went. Gathering every part of him in its debris field, with only one intent. To destroy.

Before he knew what he was doing, Dan had gotten back into the car and began the short drive into town, to the place where he knew his wife was doing something he didn't want her to be doing.

The journey passed in a haze. Later on, he would not even be able recall getting in the car let alone driving it anywhere. He parked on the street just down from the community centre, where the bulk of the preparations were being held. Daylight was already beginning to ebb as he arrived, and the brightest glow came from the windows. Smiling people illuminated, gathered together, holding mugs of coffee, poring over tables covered in material and craft supplies. Adults and children alike holding out costumes to try on, raising homemade lanterns amid gasps of delight. It was enough to make him sick.

One child, no more than eleven years old, had dressed in the garb of a punch and judy styled devil. A glorious deep red mask with a hooked nose and smiling eyes beneath a hat made of coarse linen. He saw the others turn and point, revelling in their play acting. Oh how they laughed and threw up their hands in mock horror at this terrible vision before them.

Then he caught sight of her. Grace. At one end of the room, holding a mug in one hand and laughing with a person who had their back to him. She faced the window, it was too dark outside now for her to see him, but he could see how happy she looked. She reminded him of the woman he'd first met, the Grace of old. The young, carefree girl he'd fallen for, always laughing or singing with that sparkle in her eye that made his heart skip a beat. He'd missed that about her in recent years. Was that his fault? she'd become sombre, and quiet. A wave of guilt drowned him. She'd be better off without him, wouldn't she? That beautiful, warm, caring woman in there. The woman who would leave him soon, regardless.

He couldn't bring himself to do it. How could he destroy her happiness yet again? The earth rolled beneath his feet and his stomach turned to ice. He spun on his heels to leave but a sudden voice made him jump. A whisper so close he'd swear he felt hot breath against his skin. Whipping his head about he could see noone, but there at that exact moment Grace was once more within sight, and a man who was obviously very pleased to see her opened his arms to her and she stepped forward into his embrace.

That surge of anger returned in an instant and without a second thought he made for the door of the building, heaving it open, he rudely pushed past the surprised folks within. "Grace!" he called. "Grace…I need to talk to you!"

She turned to the sound of his voice, surprised but smiling. "Dan, you came? This is Steve…he's the director of - "

"I need to speak to you Grace. Outside!" He growled, with not even a slight acknowledgment of Steve, nor the people surrounding them. Grace's smile vanished. She made a brief apology to her companions and followed Dan out to the car. They got in and he slammed his door.

"What's wrong with you?" She hissed.

"What's wrong with me? Are you joking? What are you doing with that bloke in there? Hugging and giggling like you're on some sort of date. Did you forget you're actually married? And what have you been talking to my Mother about? What happens in our house has nothing to do with anyone… Do you hear me? It's no one's business but ours!"

"What are you talking about? I called Jan

because I wondered if she could tell me any more about your Uncle! I think I was entitled to let her know the kind of things he was up to at the very least. It's not like you ever bother to speak to her these days! And after everything she's done for us... And as for Steve... wow! Just.. wow! I knew you had a jealous streak Daniel, but I didn't realise you'd become quite so irrational."

"Irrational?" He shouted.

"Yes. Irrational. I think you should go home and sleep this off."

"You think I'm drunk now?"

Grace stared at him, utterly lost. "Why else would you be behaving like this? Tell me? It's not like you Dan."

His face was cold, expressionless. Grace waited for his response, eyes pleading but he continued to look straight out of the windscreen, ignoring her, so she quietly got out of the car and walked back inside the community centre. She paused at the door only to watch as her Husband started up the car and sped away.

Hours later, the sound of car tyres crunching on the gravel drive startled Daniel back to wakefulness. He jumped up from the sofa and peered furtively out the kitchen window. He watched Grace exit the passenger side and move around to the driver's window. Steve had dropped her home. Of course he had. Dan rolled his eyes and seethed. He watched them say their farewell and only when Grace was inside and the car pulled away did he step out into the hallway.

"You startled me!" She muttered, hanging her jacket on the coat rack. She refused to look him in the eye.

"Was that him?"

She sighed. "Please just drop this Dan. I'm not going to have another pointless fight."

He raised his voice a notch. "Pointless? I don't see our marriage as pointless, but I guess it's nice to know that you do!" He was spoiling for a fight and he didn't even know why.

"I'm going to have a bath now." She spoke in such a tone as to pacify a small child having a tantrum.

"You're walking away from me then? You won't sort this out?"

She pushed past him and took the stairs at a leisurely pace. Wearied from so much drama. Dan fumed. He noted that in her haste to escape him she'd left her bag on the hall table, her phone next to it. A text message beeped, illuminating the screen. "Everything OK?" It was from him again. Dan picked up the phone and darted a look up the stairs. He could hear the water running. He glared at the message again, but placed the phone back he'd found it.

He noticed she'd been shopping too. A paper carrier bag contained some lumpy looking objects. Christmas decorations. "Some fucking Christmas this is!" He muttered, kicking over the bag, spilling its glittery contents onto the floor. He gave it another kick for good measure gaining some small sense of petty satisfaction at the sound of shattering baubles. Leaning down to examine his destruction one of the brightly coloured baubles rolled out. His name was written in decorative script around it, and there in the bag was another with Grace, also in swirly writing. The others had similarly romantic words and imagery of home and hearth. A vision of a perfect family Christmas. Grace's vision.

Guilt flooded his being as he realised what he'd done, yet again, without intending to. He was slowly destroying his marriage, and his life and yet he felt compelled to do these things. But why? A sense of panic overcame him and he ran for the car and headed to the DIY store, desperately hoping that it was still open.

Grace lay in the hot water, soaking her aching body. Everything hurt lately, not just from the new job or the extra walking they'd been doing, but from the mental exhaustion too. Every muscle was permanently tensed, awaiting the next fight or piece of unpleasant news. How much longer could they even go on like this? She feared that perhaps things were so close to the end, and that she had no more tears to shed.

She'd heard Dan leave and didn't even care where he'd gone. Eventually she pulled herself up out of the cooling bathwater, wrapped herself in a thick fleece dressing gown and headed downstairs. She stopped dead at the kitchen door, where the bag of decorations had been hastily stuffed back together. The strings of tinsel were slightly worse for wear and the shards of coloured glass on the floor told her what she would find inside the bag. A sense of emptiness filled her, a hollow detachment where she ought to have felt rage, sadness, hurt… but there was nothing. She left the pathetic remnants of the bag as it was, made herself a mug of tea and took it upstairs to bed. She paid no attention when she heard Dan return and start dragging things about downstairs. Hoping that whatever he was up to she wouldn't be left to clean up the mess tomorrow. Eventually, Dan shouted up the stairs, jolting her from a quiet doze.

"Grace? Grace! Can you come downstairs please? I want to show you something."

She considered ignoring him, but didn't have the energy for another fight. She trudged despondently down the stairs, wondering what distressing sight she would meet at the bottom.

Dan stood eagerly in the hall by the lounge door, nervously fidgeting. "Grace. I… err… I accidentally fell over your bag of Christmas decorations - "

"I noticed." She responded flatly.

"So I got you some more… and… Ta Daaaah!" He stepped away from the door with his arms out as though he were practising to be some sort of idiotic game show host, in order to reveal a fully decked out lounge complete with Christmas tree.

"OH!" She gasped. "Bloody hell... you were feeling guilty!" She muttered sarcastically under her breath as she surveyed the room. "A real tree?"

"Yeh, it's only a small one, but they didn't have much else left. I guess people buy their trees early here."

"I mean... I ...don't think it's that early. " Grace stammered. "There's less than a fortnight to go, but..."

Dan grinned expectantly at her, as if one tiny gesture could undo every argument and every upset he'd caused these past months. The gratitude she wanted to feel stuck in her throat like a dry old crumb of bread. She was tired of the drama, and knew that with every apology came more heartache, but even now, she couldn't be the one to ruin this moment, so she just smiled.

"I even put your first present under the tree." He gestured to the glittery gift bag that was overflowing conspicuously with coloured tissue paper.

"Ah..." Grace nodded. "I suppose I'll have to buy you something now." She glanced sideways at his dismayed expression. "I'm kidding. They're in a box under the bed. I'll put them out later."

Daniel pulled her close and wrapped his arms around her. He said nothing, but the tightness of the squeeze said more than words ever could, but even so, Grace was beginning to tire of this merry go round. There's only so many times a person can paper over the cracks before the whole wall crumbles to dust.

CHAPTER 13 - BOUND BY CHAOS

Grace found her husband standing forlornly in the ruin that had previously been the spare bedroom. "Dan? Oh. You're in here."

Barely aware of her peering around the doorway, he offered up the vague, watery smile of the perpetually distracted.

"I'm off to work for the lunchtime shift today, but... Ummm." She hesitated uncomfortably before taking a breath that couldn't disguise the apprehension in her voice. "I wanted to go and help with the Wintertide prep straight from work. It'll only be a couple of hours. Are you OK with that?"

Dan glared mercilessly at the floor in utter shame. "I'm a dickhead, I know it. And I'm sorry. You don't have to ask for my permission."

"I know I don't. But nor do I want you coming up to the community centre and upsetting people. It's not fair on them, or the kids."

"I know... I know..." He muttered. "I won't. Take the car, that way you don't need to wait for me."

"You sure?"

"Yes. I'll do some bits in the house. Need to get my website back online, find some new clients. I can't live on savings forever."

Grace blinked in surprise, it had been a year since he'd closed his web design business. There had been too much else going on in his head to concentrate and he'd lost a few fairly big contracts. It might be a good sign that he was thinking of starting things up again though. "Sounds like a good idea! I bet I could get you your first new client. My boss keeps talking about re-doing the restaurant's website but she hasn't had time, and to be honest she never will. I think she's been saying that for the last twelve months!"

"Great!" Dan perked up. "Tell her she can have 'mates rates!"

"OK, I'll see what I can do." She hung in the doorway a moment longer than necessary. "Dan?"

"Mmm?"

"Will you be OK?"

He knew what she was really asking, and it wasn't something he could realistically answer. "Yeah, of course. Have a good shift, and enjoy yourself later."

Lunchtime arrived far quicker than Daniel had realised, having lost at least an hour to staring at the gaping hole in the old fireplace. His plans to tidy things up or perhaps finish off some of the other small jobs around the house had evaporated.

Nor was he truly hungry and the idea of food was more of a distraction technique than anything, but when a rummage in the fridge came up empty his mind turned to the pub. Perhaps he could grab something to eat there, and sink a few beers. Judging it the only sensible option, he set off immediately.

Rain had fallen again overnight but the pavements simply refused to dry out. Apparently it was true what they said, Cornish winters were mild and humid, which in reality was far less appealing than it might sound. The aroma of damp feet and wet dog rose from his surroundings to mingle with woodsmoke and the waft of beer as he swung open the pub doors.

The pub was bustling but not so busy that he couldn't find a quiet table in the corner near the bar. He ordered a pint and some fish and chips from an older man he'd not seen before. The tall, cheery looking chap returned from the kitchen to pour Dan's pint and, as someone who is used to putting strangers at ease, he called out. "You local?"

To which Dan replied. "Yes! My Wife and I just moved here from London, actually."

"Ah, I lived up Country for a few years, hated it! Missed the beaches, and the slower way of life. Everyone's in such a rush up there!" He brought Dan's drink to the table and hovered. "Yeah, can't beat it. But you'll either love it or hate it down here.

Some folks move down and never leave, but others, they just can't settle. Too quiet for them, or too far from the big Cities. How are you finding it so far?" He inquired.

Dan nodded thoughtfully and took a large sip of his beer. "From what we've seen so far, I think we're pretty lucky to be honest! My Wife just got a job and we're doing up the house. Yeah, we've had a few bumps but… I think it will work out."

The barman grinned, lithely nipping back behind the bar to clean some glasses. "Glad to hear it! We're all friendly round here, some of them moan about the emmets, but once they realise you're here to stay you'll fit right in."

"Emits?"

"Ah, yeah, it's what we affectionately call the tourists." He laughed. "Bit of a love-hate relationship, but they're mostly nice people, some of them come back year after year. Always nice to see familiar faces."

Dan chuckled along with him. "I never realised I'd have to learn a new language to live here!"

"Won't take you long, we'll have you sounding like a proper Cornishman in no time!" he guffawed.

Just then a familiar figure strolled in through the door.

"Terry!" The barman called. "The usual?"

"Aye." Muttered the gruff middle aged man as he meandered towards them, giving Dan a wary nod in greeting.

"Have you met our new local, Tel?" The barman said, turning belatedly to ask Dan his name.

Terry replied slowly. "I have indeed Chris, I have indeed."

Dan grinned awkwardly, as his meal was brought out, taking the opportunity to shovel a large forkful of fish into his mouth, absolving him of any further responsibility to make polite conversation.

Terry leaned forward, his elbows on the edge of the bar, as Chris rapidly filled him in on the latest comings and goings as if they were an old married couple.

Dan listened intently as he munched. Between them, the men seemed to know the entire village's comings and goings. Whoever said it was only Women that gossip, was very much mistaken. Suddenly, in amongst the mindless tattling, the barman said something that made Dan's food go down the wrong way.

"Aye, that Blackthorn fellow was hanging about again. Strange old bugger." Said Chris with his deeply Cornish accent, rolling the rrr's as he spoke.

Terry gave a rumble of agreement.

"Anna says he gives her the creeps. Can't say I blame her. Not seen him around so much since John passed. I've heard rumours that the old fella knows more about his death than he let on!"

Terry gave a shifty glance at Daniel and coughed. "Yeah, well I don't know too much about all that."

Daniel pushed his plate to one side, picked up his almost empty glass, and walked to the bar for a refill. "Is this John Padget you're talking about?"

"Aye it is. Familiar with him, are you?" Chris responded.

"Yes." Daniel tried to catch Terry's eye. "He was my Uncle. I inherited his house."

Terry coughed again, and Chris swung to meet Dan's gaze, his mouth hung open in astonishment. "OH! Oh, well…" He muttered. "My condolences, I had no idea you were John's nephew."

"Thanks. I didn't really know him to be honest, as he turned his back on family when I was a kid. I'd be interested to hear what you know of it all though. I've come across that Mr Blackthorn myself, and found him to be a bit…" His mind searched frantically for the least offensive word possible.

Chris snorted, one eyebrow raised and Terry chuckled into his beer.

"He said he knew Uncle John, but wouldn't elaborate. Wittered on about not seeing him for a while, said he stopped going out."

"Well that's true." Said Terry. "The last few months before he… passed, he'd become a bit of a recluse."

Daniel took a sip of his drink. "How come?"

Terry sighed, clearly reluctant to speak on this topic. Chris gave him a nudge. "Go on Terry, the lad surely has a right to know."

"John always liked a drink or two, he was a regular in here. Most people knew him and liked him. Once or twice there was a lady on his arm, but they never seemed to last. I'm not saying there was anything wrong with him ya know, just, well some people are better on their own aren't they?"

Chris muttered an agreement and ducked away to serve a new customer.

Terry shifted his weight to find a more comfortable stance. "Anyway, something must have happened a few years back, he disappeared for a few months. Locked up the house and vanished. Then he just showed up out of the blue one day, seemed like he was drinking to drown his sorrows if you ask me. And from then on he never stopped!"

Chris had returned eagerly to the tale. "He sure could put 'em away. Had to refuse to serve him once or twice!" He winced.

Daniel rolled his eyes at the way this was going. "So he was a drunk! Typical."

Terry took a cautious sip from his pint. "Well, it can get to any man I suppose, and he didn't have anyone at home to help him do anything else. And that Blackthorn fella, he didn't help matters." He turned to Chris, behind the bar, "I don't recall ever seeing him before that. Do you?"

"Old Blackthorn? Nope, can't say I can."

Terry continued, well into his tale now. "P'rhaps there was more to them than met the eye, but while John was downing drinks like a fish, I never saw that other fella so much as finish a pint." He shook his head in dismay. "Over time Johnny grew more aggressive, and wouldn't let anyone near. D'you remember when Angie found him passed out down on the beach that day? " Both men shook their heads in unison. "He nearly went for her, and all because she was trying to see if he needed help. Well, no one tried again after that. Left him to it. Not much you can do for someone when they've decided on a path like that."

Chris leaned in closer and added softly, "People wondered if he'd, ya know… started to lose his marbles. I mean, he wasn't that old, but…he clearly wasn't quite right. Can't say if it was the drink that tipped him, or something else. He came in here one day raving about demons and hell, and lord knows what else!"

A cold shiver went down Dan's spine. "Demons?"

"Yeah, in a right state he was. Kept trying to tell people that he was being chased by the devil. In a bad way, he was. Didn't see him much after that, did you Tel'?"

Terry pondered, "Once or twice. He wasn't a well man though."

"So what happened then?" Dan pushed, feeling a sudden desire to keep the conversation flowing. "Can I get you another drink?"

"Cheers, I will. Not that I feel good about sharing bad news about your family."

Dan replied quickly. "Don't feel bad. You're doing me a favour, and to be honest, while we're at it I should apologise for being such a dick to you last time we met. I... err.. had a lot on my plate that day."

To his credit Terry held up a hand in acknowledgment of the apology, gracefully brushing it aside. "No explanation needed my friend. I took no offence."

"Well, I appreciate that. And please, go on! You're actually answering a few questions I had about him too. This explains a lot."

The men frowned, curiously wondering what more there would be to this story, but Terry forged reluctantly on. "To be fair I didn't really speak to him, I'd see him now and then when I was walking the dog. Heard a few unpleasant rumours. Not that I'd want to speculate, mind."

"What sort of rumours? Dan urged.

Terry seemed visibly uncomfortable. "Oh silly things... some family pets went missing. Bloomin' cats, you know what those creatures are like, they come and go as they please, but word got round that they'd last seen one of 'em up at John's place." He shuffled a bit. "Well they started saying he was stealing animals."

Chris interrupted. "Not just stealing them, killing them! Warding off evil with weird sacrifices and stuff."

"Because of the devil chasing him?" Dan asked.

Chris turned to fetch a drink for another customer but raised his voice to continue the conversation. "Oh yes, that and the fact he'd drawn all those devil symbols all over the place!"

"What?" Daniel nearly choked on his drink. "You mean he painted those things on the gate post himself?" He turned to Terry in amazement. "You didn't tell me that!"

"Well now," Terry fidgeted. "It didn't seem right to, at the time."

"Fair enough, I didn't really give you much of a chance I guess…" Daniel muttered. "I can't believe it!"

"He had a lot of people concerned for his well being, sad thing is that he just didn't want it. Locked himself away and well, it's said he took his own life. Not up at the house, mind…" Terry added, hurriedly. "Fell in the river up near Highertown, apparently. Probably drunk." He tutted.

"Most likely, that's what they say." Chris agreed.

Dan was stunned by the revelations. It would explain a lot about the macabre things they'd found at the house, but still… What did any of this have to do with Tom?

"Did either of you ever see him with another man? Younger, looks a bit like me?"

They looked at each other and back to Dan. "Nope, don't think so."

"Only, my older Brother went missing a year or so ago. Police couldn't find him, but when we moved into the house, John's house.. I found his bag. My brother's rucksack and clothes…"

"Well now!" Terry exclaimed. "There's a thing!"

"What's his name?" Asked Chris.

"Tom. Hang on, I have a picture on my phone…"

The men scratched their chins and muttered, but could not recall having ever seen Tom before. Daniel's heart sank. He had seemed so close to discovering the truth, and now all he had were even more questions.

"What about at the funeral? Anyone you didn't recognise?"

The men exchanged another glance. "Weren't no funeral." Terry muttered. "We just seemed to hear about it all after the fact. Strange that!"

"Well I mean, he didn't have any family to organise it did he?" Chris added, looking a little embarrassed.

"That's weird. I wonder why we weren't contacted?" Daniel said. "They got in touch afterwards to tell me that I'd inherited his house, but not to inform us of his death?" his question hung there, suspended in the air. Unanswered.

CHAPTER 14 - SECRETS

Grace returned home that evening full of beans, but dead on her feet. She collapsed onto the sofa, with an exhausted, but happy groan.

"Good day then?" Dan asked, handing her a mug of tea.

"It was actually. Work was ok. A bit rushed off my feet, but…ah, I don't mind and they're nice people. And we had so much fun at the festival prep, oh Dan, I hope you'll come with me to watch it. I'll knock off work and go straight there. The parade comes all the way down to Penmeryn, it's going to look incredible!"

He grinned. It was nice to see her so happy for a change, but the twinge of jealousy stung more than he'd care to admit. "Yeah, of course I will."

"So what did you get up to today?" She asked.

"Well… I went to the pub for lunch and ended up having drinks with our neighbour Terry, and Chris, he works there. Nice bloke!"

"Wow, you've been out socialising? I hope you were nice to them…"

"Of course I was! I apologised to Terry for our last conversation. He said it was fine."

"Miracles do happen! I'm glad, that makes me very happy." She smiled.

"Yeah, they had some interesting tales to tell of old Uncle John."

"Really?"

"Yeah, it seems he had a few issues with his mental health. He became an alcoholic and had a bit of a breakdown. It seems he painted that stuff on the gatepost himself."

"No way!" Grace sat up straighter in the chair, mug clasped to her knee. "Well that would explain a few things!"

"That's exactly what I said." Dan replied. "I did ask if they'd seen him with Tom."

"No luck?"

He shook his head.

"It was worth asking." She leaned over and grabbed his hand, pulling him down to sit beside her. "Maybe things can start to settle down now. We've got Christmas to look forward to, and the festival, and your business getting back up and running - Oh, by the way, am I a good sales rep or what?" She blew on her knuckles and shined them on her sleeve, grinning smugly. "I got you the restaurant contract. And... maybe, if you want to do it... the Winterfest website. I mean, there's not much to put on it for most of the year but they have fundraisers and advertising, and they want a message board added to keep in touch with volunteers."

"Steady on… I'm gonna have to start paying you at this rate!" He laughed. "Thanks Grace. What would I do without you?"

"You really want me to answer that?"

"Nah…"

"But if you really want to show your appreciation you could get me a cheeky glass of Baileys, make it a large one though!"

"Oh someone's feeling festive! You've been playing your Christmas music compilations in the car again haven't you?"

"Nothing wrong with a bit of Wham!"

"It's not Wham I object to, it's bloody Take That! In some marriages that sort of taste in music would be grounds for divorce!" He called back over his shoulder, still laughing, as he filled two glasses with ice and rummaged in the booze cupboard. "Do you want anything to eat while I'm out here?"

"No thanks. We ordered some pizzas at the community centre. Wasn't all that hungry to be honest, been feeling a bit off colour. Could use an early night really."

"Are you alright?" He asked, concerned.

"Yeah, it's probably nothing. At least I'm not at work tomorrow. I'll make a start on the Christmas food shop I think."

Daniel returned, two glasses of Baileys in hand. "Ooh, snacks… pigs in blankets?"

"Yes, *for Christmas*!" She warned. "I asked Jan if she wanted to join us but she's made plans already, but we'll get her down for New Year."

"Do you think it's my fault?"

"What? That she can't come for Christmas? Don't be silly. She's got her life back in London, she's never been short of friends. Probably having a whale of a time now her nosey son, and daughter in law are out of the way."

Daniel shrugged, "I s'pose." But he knew he'd often pushed his Mother's patience to the limit, as he did with everyone he loved apparently, and he wondered if he'd ever get a chance to make it up to them.

The following days passed relatively peacefully. Almost normal, one could say, although *normal* was something so out of the ordinary these days, that it felt strangely *abnormal*. They moved through their daily lives with a sense of uneasy anticipation, as though waiting for the other shoe to drop. Because even they knew the calm could not last.

Daniel had set up his PC and made a start on the web design business. After a brief moment of panic that he'd forgotten how to do it, all his years of knowledge came flooding back and for a time he found some sense of peace in something to occupy his scattered, fragile thoughts. One morning, he opened his emails to send a quick message to a new client and spotted something he did not expect. It was an automated reply from the web forum he'd signed up to, in order to contact that guy who seemed to know something about the weird symbols. All thoughts of work fled as he opened the message. It was brief, but to the point. "Hi. If you have any connection with this symbol, walk away mate. Walk away. Don't get involved. Sorry."

Dan stared at the words as if they might make more sense the longer he looked at them, but of course they didn't. "Walk away? Great. Really useful buddy. Thanks!"

He clicked back to his work document and stared blindly at the screen. "Come on Dan... get a grip. You've got work to do. Focus!"

But then, as if he needed more interruptions his phone beeped as a text rudely announced itself. It was from Ellie. He hadn't thought they'd ever hear from her again after their last encounter, but here she was, asking to speak to him. *Urgently.*

Things had been going so well lately, Grace seemed happy. Did he really want to start down this path yet again? Apparently so. He called her number.

"Dan?" She answered immediately.

"I didn't think there was any more to say?"

"Nor did I." She replied quietly. "Apparently I'm getting messages for you though, and when I'm told to deliver them, I do."

"Messages? From your spirits I assume?" He scoffed.

"I have to warn you…"

He nearly hung up on her there and then. "Oh another warning? There's a surprise. No we are not leaving Cornwall and running away based on a tarot reading Ellie. We've got too much to lose."

"I know that. That's why I've been told to tell you - "

"Look," He cut her off. "I've been chatting to some neighbours. My Uncle became a drunk and lost his marbles. He painted that shit on the gatepost himself. He was crazy! It's all nonsense." Silence echoed at the end of the phone. "Ellie?"

"I know that. I'd heard the rumours."

He felt a familiar flush of heat beneath his skin. "You knew? You knew and didn't think to tell us? Such a great friend you are!"

"I didn't see how it would help, and besides, I didn't know him personally. It was only a rumour, I didn't know if it was true or not."

"What *is* it you want to tell me Ellie?" He stated, so politely as to sound rude.

"You have a choice before you. You've reached a crossroads of sorts, one that will alter the rest of your life. A decision that will hang over you and your family for years, in fact it's something you may never fully escape."

"So that's it? That's the message?" He asked, scornfully.

"Choose wisely Daniel. That's all I can tell you, when the time comes, please choose wisely. They spoke to you that day, at the well. Whether you recall it or not, they gave you all the help they could. Think carefully before you make a choice.

I'm sorry, I… I hope things work out for you." The phone gave a tiny click as Ellie ended the call.

Sunday morning they awoke to heavy rain. Its hammering could be heard against the windows before either of them had so much as thought about opening the curtains."What are you up to?" Groaned Grace from beneath a cosy, warm nest. Dan was up stupidly early, pulling on his clothes with an odd sense of purpose.

"I've got something I need to do."
"Right now? In this weather?"
"I won't be long."
"Can't we just have a lie in together? Where are you going?" She asked, suddenly feeling a little concerned.

"Don't worry about it. I'll be back soon and we'll go for a roast at the pub." He leaned over to kiss the top of her head.

"But Dan?"

"I'll tell you later, I promise. I just need to do this… while I can." He rushed from the room leaving the door ajar. Grace listened to his footfall on the stairs, the zip of his coat, the jingle of keys, the slam of the front door behind him. She fell back into the shape of her pillow with a sigh. Last night had been her best sleep in a long while and didn't relish dragging herself out of bed too quickly, so she lay there a bit longer, secretly hoping that Dan would return with coffee and a cheese twist. Ten minutes felt like an hour and she grew too fidgety to fall back to sleep, and the thought of coffee drove her out from beneath the duvet.

She pulled on her old, scruffy work jeans and a jumper, checking the radiator gingerly with her hand to see if it was still working. It was, but the house felt so unusually cold this morning. She pottered about, made coffee and buttered toast, and sat down to her laptop where she lost herself in conversation for a time with some of the volunteers of the Wintertide festival. It had been on all the local news channels throughout Cornwall this year, they expected a record turn out and wanted to make the lantern display something really special. Grace couldn't remember ever having such a sense of community pride before, and she was so proud to be part of something so inspirational. It was just a shame that Dan couldn't seem to share this with her though. It wasn't that she felt lonely, only that she'd hoped this move would bring the two of them closer, and yet it was almost as if everything that happened conspired to drive them further apart.

The hours ticked by and Grace realised she'd been sitting there far longer than originally planned. She flicked the kettle on to boil for a cup of tea, and wandered through to the lounge, where she was reminded of the huge mound of ashes and blackened shards of wood in the fireplace.

Returning moments later with a dustpan and brush, she gave it a thorough clean and had soon restacked the logs ready for their next cosy blaze.

Daniel still had not returned. Grace checked her phone. It was now gone midday. She sent him a text. *"Everything alright? xx"*

No reply came, so she switched on a table lamp, picked up her book and decided to try and enjoy the peace and quiet for a while.

The rain fell continuously, like a wall of water cascading down an invisible rock face. It's muddy grey hue filtered through the raindrops on the window, invading the room itself. The whole world felt damp and gloomy. Even her bones felt soggy. She couldn't concentrate on her book and eventually, having read the same page about five times over, she relented, and checked her phone again. Concern turned to annoyance. What was he thinking, just dashing off like that? That's the trouble, he didn't think. Ever!

Placing her book on the coffee table, she glanced up out of the window to see him standing there, beneath the magnolia tree. *Daniel?* She froze. No, it wasn't Daniel, but it was a man… or perhaps the shadow of a man, dark shapes where a man ought to be. She blinked, heart thumping too loudly within her rib cage. She rubbed her eyes thinking they were out of focus, but they weren't, her eyesight was just fine. It was the man shadow thing that was out of focus. She tried to move closer to the window, but a stinging sensation like pins and needles sliced through her feet and legs causing her to stumble. Reaching down to rub painful calf muscles, she looked back out at the tree. The shadow was gone.

She pressed her brow against the cold pane of glass to see further into the garden. There were no intruders. Nothing, except the grey rain running in rivulets down the window, dripping from plants and drainpipes and fencing alike, with a steady *drip.. drip...drip...*

She snatched up her phone to call Daniel. This was getting ridiculous now, what could he possibly be doing for all this time, out in this weather? The dial tone buzzed, she knew what it would sound like, he had his favourite Battlestar Galactica ringtone set for her incoming calls, but he did not pick up. She gave it a few minutes then tried again before it went straight to voicemail. The phone in her hand shook a little. He'd probably waltz back in and laugh at her for being worried, but she couldn't help it. Something Just didn't feel right.

She paced the room, nervously checking outside again. It was already getting dark, daylight hadn't even bothered to put in an appearance today. She stared at her phone again, willing it to ring, then in desperation she pressed Ellie's number. The hollow of Grace's chest burned with anxiety.

"Hello?"

"Ellie. I'm sorry to bother you, but do you happen to know where Dan is?" The quiver in her voice gave her away.

"No. What's happened?"

"He left early this morning saying he had to do something, and he wouldn't say where he was going. I've been trying to call him but he won't pick up. I… I just thought… I just wondered if he'd talked to you?"

Ellie paused for a moment. "Is that all he said?" She asked.

Grace tried to recall his words from hours ago, the last time she'd seen him. "He said he had to do something… while he still could. I don't understand any of it."

"OK, hold on, I'll come over and we can go look for him. I may have an idea."

Thirty minutes later Ellie beeped the horn of her Land Rover. Grace had been ready for ages, pacing the hallway. She ran through the rain to join her. "I'm sorry to drag you out in this."

"Don't be silly."

"So where do you think he is?"

"It's just a guess, but he may have gone back to the well."

"That strange place with the clootie tree? Why would he do that?"

"I told him to return the offering."

"What offering?"

Ellie looked surprised. "The key. He didn't

show it to you?"

"I've no idea what you're talking about."

"He confessed to me that he'd found a key on the floor of the well, after he'd thrown the pebble into the pool - "

"- But he said nothing happened!"

"Yeah. He lied. And when I warned him that you should be careful and leave the house, I also told him it might be wise to return the key. Just in case."

Grace seemed so out of her depth. "I don't understand any of this Ellie. I know you've only tried to help, but I'm sorry we ever got you involved."

Ellie didn't waste time driving all the way to the official car park, but pulled in amongst the trees on the curb side. "It's a short cut." She muttered. They hastily got out and picked their way up a steep bank which somehow halved their journey to reach the ominous clootie tree, which from this angle loomed over them like some ragged war torn guardian angel making its final stand.

They ran as quickly as they could manage, given the swamp-like conditions, towards the clearing, Grace frantically scanned her surroundings. "He's not here!" She panted. "DANIEL?" She called in desperation.

Ellie, meanwhile, headed straight for the well and took the steps into the sacred cavern two at a time. "Grace? Down here…"

Grace followed Ellie's voice back into the familiar darkness, to find her standing completely still, the light from her phone illuminated a figure that seemed to fill the small chamber with a solid black shadow that spread outwards and along the walls, almost to its very edges.

"Daniel?"

He didn't move, so she stepped closer, reaching out a hand towards him. "Daniel?"

He'd become a statue, an animal caught in the beams of a headlight. Staring straight ahead at nothing in particular.

"What the fuck is wrong with him?" Grace whispered. Almost scared to touch him in case it spooked him and he fell into the water.

Ellie moved to his side and together they took hold of his arms. He jumped, terrified, eyes wide as saucers.

"WHAT?"

"Dan, it's ok, it's just me… Grace. And Ellie's with me. We came to find you."

"Grace?" He whispered. Fear edged his voice, but there was something else in the way he spoke. Something she'd never heard before.

"Come up the steps Dan, we'll get you home." She murmured softly.

"I had to come. I had to…"

"Tell me about it later Dan, please, just be careful… let's get you to the car."

Between them, they managed to guide him

back down to the car, how they made it there in one piece, Grace would never know. The rain fell and the mud was black and slick. The Clootie tree watched them leave with skeletal arms outstretched, ribbons and prayer flags skewered by thorns and stained. Tattered, torn and ragged beyond repair, but held fast by any means possible.

CHAPTER 15 - THE HOUSE ON THE CROSSROADS

Daniel slept like the dead throughout the next day. Ellie had taken Grace to retrieve the car, but she'd also stayed off work to be there when he awoke. When he finally did, he recalled very little.

"What were you doing there?" Grace asked.

Struggling, he tried to think clearly. "I don't know, I don't even remember getting there."

"You ran out of here at the crack of dawn saying you had to do something while you still could. When I couldn't get hold of you by the afternoon I was worried, I called Ellie in case she knew where you were. She seemed to think you'd gone to give back a key or something? What's that all about?"

"The key?" He looked panicked. "Where is it?" He scrambled to reach for his clothes, pulled the pockets inside out.

"Dan, what are you doing? What's so important about a key?"

He sat on the floor, staring at his pile of clothes scattered across the carpet. "I don't know...

I need it."

Something inside Grace broke. "Everytime I think things are finally settling down, something like this happens." She sobbed into her hands. "I'm so tired. I can't take much more of this Dan. I'm sorry but I really can't. We can't deal with this alone."

He got to his feet. "I don't know how to stop it. I don't even feel like I have any control of what I'm doing."

"You just need to get some help." She begged
"I will. I promise."

But they both knew it was a hollow promise. Whatever this was, whatever path he was on, they knew deep down that they would have no choice but to ride it through to the bitter end.

Grace returned reluctantly to work, Daniel dropped her off in an attempt to convince her that he was well enough to be left alone. He had planned to spend the day working on his new client's website and doing some admin jobs. He'd promised Grace that he would make another appointment with the Doctors surgery too.

The drive home felt good. In his mind he was finally doing something worthwhile again. He would throw himself back into his work, build up a new portfolio, and get some builders round in the New Year to get the house properly sorted out. He smiled as he drove, making plans for the week, and for the future.

Sitting down at his computer with a fresh cup of coffee, he scanned his *To Do* list. The new site for the restaurant was coming along nicely, he'd called in a favour with an old graphic designer buddy from college who had created a stunning new logo for them. He was really excited to get it finished, just the forum to lay out now and it would be ready to go live. He looked forward to seeing Grace's face when she saw what an effort he'd made on it. But as he flicked open his internet browser he saw a tab left open with a map of Carn Madrow. It caught his attention and he found himself zooming in to see where they had walked the other week. The stones were clearly marked and he made out the rough track they had followed, but just off to the left, about halfway along, there appeared to be a second path. One he did not recall.

Viewing it on the map, it formed a crossroads, with the stone circle occupying the land in its top right quarter, and a small building lower down. He sat back and stared out of the window, as he tried to recall having seen anything else there. The path was obviously overgrown, but there hadn't been a building there, he was certain.

He thought back to what Ellie had said about the crossroads in mythology, and that she'd told him the image Uncle John had painted outside was symbolic of a crossroads… and not forgetting that this very house was also built on a crossroads. The connection bothered him, but mostly because he just couldn't figure out what it all meant.

He forced his attention back to the computer, closing the browser window with its tantalising mysteries, and refocused on work. He squirmed in his seat, his gaze kept wandering, finally he got up to make another cup of coffee, restlessly pacing the kitchen while the kettle boiled. He just couldn't get that map out of his head. It's only half an hour away, he could go over there for a breather and a quick look around, he told himself. Grace wouldn't even need to know. He talked himself out of it at least four times before pouring the freshly made coffee into a travel mug and pulling on his walking boots, still caked in mud from his previous foray into the unknown.

Parking in the same spot as before he strode off at a far more confident pace in the direction of the stone circle, with a screenshot of the map location, just in case he struggled to find an internet signal out here. The grass was still wild and overgrown, but just as he caught sight of the sentinel stone, peeking over the horizon, he saw it. The one thing he had missed the last time. A low lying waymarker, carved into a stone and placed at the centre of the crossroads. The disused pathways were hard to make out, but not impossible and so he followed this new track through a small hedge of brambles and hawthorn to a disused field, now just full of weeds and overgrown rubble. And there, right in the centre of his view was a dilapidated farmhouse.

The wind whistled annoyingly, past his ears and dust blew into his eyes, making them sting. The stone circle was most definitely visible from this vantage point, so why he'd not noticed the farmhouse was beyond him. A lone Crow flapped noisily down to sit atop the shabby roof and judge him haughtily. It spread its coal black feathers wide in some sort of display that Daniel didn't quite grasp, then, opening its beak wide, it gave a deep and ominous *Cawww* that vibrated ominously, through the ground beneath him.

"Well thanks for that Mr Crow" Daniel said. "Hopefully that means come on in, have a cup of tea… and not, set one foot in my house and I'll peck your eyes out!" He glared at the creature, which still watched him closely, beady eyes glinting mischievously.

Drawing level with the narrow, single storey building, he could see how neglected it was. From the base of the hill it could be mistaken for a livable homestead, but on closer inspection it was clear that one side was a total ruin, with an entire room exposed to the elements. Old roof timbers had collapsed and lay rotting in amongst the rubble and weeds that had now taken root there. Strangely though, the interior door leading to the rest of the house was still intact, and still firmly closed. Daniel peered in through a window at what seemed to be an old fashioned kitchen with butler sink and stone worktops. Basic and sparse, but otherwise sound, if you didn't count the rotting woodwork, ancient, crumbling plaster, and the old bird's nest that spilled from the fireplace.

The Crow launched itself from the roof to settle on the ground, just far enough to be out of reach, but close enough to continue spying on him. He eyed it suspiciously and kept walking around to the back of the building. The Crow waddled erratically behind him. "Fuck off bird! You're making me nervous..." Dan waved his hands at it, but the Crow just flapped its wings and hopped closer. "Go away!" He yelled again, almost tripping over yet more rubble which he supposed was the remnants of a wall that had once surrounded the little cottage. Most of the stone had obviously been stolen by locals over the years, and used elsewhere, but a single row of granite blocks still marked out the boundary of where it had once been.

The Crow had evidently lost interest and decided that Daniel would not be leading him to anything worthwhile after all, and with one final, deafening shout, it rose into the sky, circled him once, and made off in the direction of the stones. Daniel gave it a filthy look as it made its overly dramatic exit, and he sat down on the sturdiest part of the wall to rest a moment. He sneaked another look towards Carn Madrow again. There it was, that creepy stone leering at him across the landscape. He could almost hear its thoughts. Sense its quiet, but venomous disdain.

He pulled his phone out again to study the map. This place was mildly interesting, but now that he was here, it was far less of an exciting discovery than he'd hoped it would be. He sighed, and stood up, thinking to head back down to the car when he caught sight of a deep footprint in a patch of glistening mud by the wall. Not human, but animal. He followed the neat little row of indents back to its source. They appeared to begin at the wall and vanish into the stoney, moss covered ground beyond. He crouched to see them better. Even to his untrained city boy eyes they looked like small hoof prints! He scanned the horizon for signs of goats or grazing sheep. Not even a wild pony. Not so much as a whiff of shit. To be fair, besides that Crow, there were no signs of life at all.

He strolled the perimeter, kicking small rocks as he went until he reached the front door again. Right back where he started. He looked down to give the rock another nudge forward with his foot and stopped. There was another mark, another strange hoof print. He hadn't noticed it before, but then he hadn't been looking at the ground. An odd sensation like cold, clammy fingers tickled his spine. "Right dumbass, it's time to go home and forget all about this place!" He muttered, shoving his phone into his coat pocket and turning towards the path, but there in front of him on the ground, was a box. Not a large box, but big enough to be noticed. Large enough to know that it hadn't been there when he'd walked up to the house.

He took a few steps towards it, eyeing his surroundings suspiciously. Someone had to be fucking with him. The box was black and had no markings whatsoever. He picked it up, turned it over. It looked strangely similar to the one he'd found in Tom's rucksack, except this one had an opening. A tiny catch that he flicked, causing a lid to pop open. "What the fuck?" He stared inside at the contents for a long while as his insides slowly turned to liquid. It seemed to Dan that he stood there a lifetime before finding the courage to reach inside and touch the battered old enamel badge he'd last seen pinned to his old rucksack that he had thrown in the bin along with the rest of Tom's possessions.

Blood drummed in his ears and he thought he might throw up. He sank to his knees, hands trembling uncontrollably, he turned the badge over and over between his fingers. There was no mistaking it. He returned it to the box and snapped the lid shut, only this time, it gave a loud click and the catch that had revealed its opening suddenly vanished. Dan turned the box over and over again, searching for a sign of that opening, but it was too well hidden. The box had become just like the one he'd seen in Tom's rucksack. Smooth and completely sealed. He sat on the cold, damp ground and placed the box by his feet. He was so confused.

Suddenly there was a sound like the slow rumble of an earthquake moving closer, Dan raised his eyes from the box to the sky as the Crow returned, only now there was a whole group of them. A *murder* of Crows, as they're known. Indeed, they made such a racket you'd have thought someone was after them, or perhaps the other way around. They flew at him, he ducked, but they scattered. Each one landing in turn until they were dotted across the bleak landscape like so many black rocks. Loud and insistent waymarkers. *Here, here… this way, no, over here.* They screamed.

Daniel snatched up the box and dragged himself to his feet. Unsure what he was meant to do with any of it. Wondering what Ellie would tell him… he reached inside his pocket and felt the familiar shape of the key. The key he'd thought he returned, or lost. "*Choose wisely*," Ellie had said. "*When the time comes, choose wisely.*" Was this what she meant? And what were his options, exactly? As if guided by the Crows, he followed his own footsteps back to the front door of the cottage. Had he tried the door? No, of course not, that would be stupid, wouldn't it? He pushed and it held fast. He pushed again, noting the worn keyhole beneath its latch. He stared at it for an age. Again Ellie's voice came back to him. "*They gave you a key, Daniel. Now*

I suppose you must find the lock it belongs to."

The Crows set up a flurry of calls as a heavy, dark cloud settled above. It was going to rain. Heavily. "What the fuck am I doing?" He muttered. "It's a ruin! I can see inside through the massive fucking hole in the wall! "You think this is funny?" he yelled to the sky. "Whoever thinks this if fucking funny, you can go fuck yourself! I'm not playing your creepy little game any longer!" He threw the key, and then the box to the ground, and walked back down the hill.

Halfway home, along the winding narrow roads, his phone rang. He searched for a layby to pull in and listened to the strange voicemail. It was from the Police, something about Tom. He was in Penzance? Dan played it back twice but he couldn't quite make out the message over all the static. Phone signals were shit out here, but it definitely mentioned Tom and an address in Chapel Street. Something made him feel uneasy though, it didn't really sound like a message from the Police, and god knows he'd spoken to them often enough, but he had to know. He had to find out if it was real.

I need to tell Grace... he thought, but in that moment he realised that she wouldn't want to know. She was so sick of all this, tired of the endless tail chasing, the wasted phone calls and the arguments. And she was right to be. No. He'd have to deal with this one on his own.

The drive didn't take long, and the sat nav,

for once, managed to direct him straight there. As afternoon became evening, the clouds parted majestically to reveal a jagged row of sunbeams that glowed so vividly that it painted the whitewashed buildings of Chapel Street in ethereal shades of orange and pink, and curious blue shadows that swept across rooftops and down alleys. The world still bustled with activity, much to Dan's surprise, as the people of Penzance went about their business. None of them the least bit interested in his comings and goings.

He left the car parked on the street outside number 52. A pretty, 18th Century stone building with white sash windows and a blue sign above the door that read, *Captain Cutters House*. The double doors, also painted turquoise, no doubt to reflect the sea views from the end of the road, were left ajar. He stepped inside, into the darkness of a narrow hallway. Doors on all sides. The scent of tobacco and stale air choked his lungs. He pushed open the door to his left, it revealed nothing but an empty room. Perhaps once a shop front. A worn beige carpet and an old fireplace, and a stain on the wall that looked like damp.

He moved further along the hallway, past a set of stairs, deeper into the murky, claustrophobic building. A figure moved in the shadows. "Ahhh, Daniel…" He whispered. "You came! I'm so glad."

Daniel stopped dead in his tracks. He didn't need daylight to know that the man he faced was none other than Mr Blackthorn. Those feral eyes glinting in the half light.

"I should have known... What do you want?" He asked. "Why all the lies and tricks?"

Mr Blackthorn eased out of the darkness to where a narrow shard of golden sunlight illuminated a patch of old carpet. Some faded antique Moroccan style rug that covered a hole in an equally faded and worn carpet.

"What do you think of my little abode, eh?" He held aloft his arms, somewhat mesmerised by his surroundings. "Such a quiet, peaceful little hovel amidst the busyness of a world that no longer cares for such things."

The carvings set into the door frames and rail that wound up the staircase were reminiscent of its Cornish harbourside legacy. Whether Pirates had walked these halls or not, the decorative ambience wished those visitors to believe they had stepped back in time nonetheless.

"You live here?" Daniel asked.

"Well, yes... and no." Grinned the elusive Mr Blackthorn. "But please, come through..." He gave a low, ridiculous bow and waved Daniel through to a small room in the rear of the building.

"Why did you lie about Tom?"

"Who says I lied?" Blackthorn offered whimsically. "You want to find your Brother, and I can help." He shrugged. "I just thought it was time we talked... officially."

Blackthorn disappeared into a small sitting room, so dingy that it seemed at first glance there were no windows. Daniel squinted his eyes adjusting to the gloom, and looked around at the slightly shabby Georgian furniture, with a marble fireplace on one wall. There was indeed a window. A very small one, its view blocked by the overgrown blooms of a Rhododendron bush outside, long dead of course, now brown and withered, a mere ghost of the glory it had once been.

Blackthorn reclined in a threadbare armchair next to the fireplace. "I wish to speak bluntly. If I may?"

Daniel nodded, seating himself cautiously.

"You have been less receptive than I'd hoped to an agreement between us. Your Uncle was so much more willing. I can see that it doesn't necessarily run in the family. Unfortunately."

Daniel had never felt so out of place. "What do you want, Blackthorn? If that is even your name?"

The man made a sound like laughter, that was less like a sound and more like smoke, that gathered in the corners of the room, swirling, seeping through the cracks in the door. "What do I want? The question is never about me, all I want is for you to… want. So the question is really, what do *you* want, Daniel? And we both know the answer to that, don't we?"

"I don't understand all these games. Why me?"

"Why not?" Blackthorn laughed again.

Daniel stood, intending to leave this crazy old bastard to his own joke, but suddenly he was there, in front of him. Standing in the ever darkening hallway blocking Daniel's only means of escape.

"Daniel." He said, coldly. "Why did you discard my gift?"

"Your what? You mean the box don't you?"

"Yes. I mean the box."

"I... I don't want to play your fucking insane games, that's why!"

"Who doesn't love a good game? Keldd loves a good game. Your dear Wife enjoys a good game, doesn't she?"

Daniel's stomach hit the floor. "Leave Grace out of this."

Blackthorn chuckled, like a splintering of oak floorboards, raspy, and riddled with woodworm.

"Grace has nothing to do with this."

"Oh come now. You know she's already made up her mind about you. Love dies so quickly once the respect goes. She pities you Daniel. And pity is a poor substitute for love. If it's real love you want, look to family. The love of a Brother. A Brother who needs you! Why waste time on a fickle woman when your true family needs you?"

Daniel realised that tears soaked his face. "Grace does love me!"

"Hmm... does she? I don't think so. At least, that's what she told me last we spoke. She does enjoy her little forays out into the wide world without you. Especially that new job of hers. She really is a hit with the regulars." He smirked.

"What are you saying? Just fucking spit it out you psycho!" Daniel shouted.

Blackthorn clutched at his chest in mock horror. "Oh my, you don't know? Never wondered about her *dear f*riend Steve? She told you that it's his family business she works for, right? And that he recommended her for the job? And that he makes sure to see to her every need. Ahhh, sweet sweet romance!" He gurgled.

"I don't believe you!" Dan yelled. "I don't! Why would you do this to me?"

"Because, Dan. Because I want your attention. Because I want you to get serious with me. Take the box Dan. Take it." He held out the small black box, still smeared with mud. "Take it and see how good things can get!"

Daniel recoiled, crouching to the floor, head in hands.

"Take it Daniel. One small sacrifice and everything you want can be revealed. What could be better than that? You agreed to play this game, there is no going back on your word now."

"I didn't agree to anything!" Dan roared. "I agreed to nothing! Whatever Tom and my Uncle were caught up in with you, I don't care! I will not play your fucked up games, whatever they are! Leave me the fuck alone… and leave my Wife alone!" And with that, he pushed past the odious

Mr Blackthorn, and ran from the building.

CHAPTER 16 - DARKEST BEFORE THE DAWN

Daniel sped away from Penzance as fast as he could. Dusk had given way to nightfall and the roads were now illuminated by row upon row of streetlights. Once back out on the main road he drove on autopilot, his thoughts raced. He didn't fully understand what was happening, except that he knew Blackthorn, or Keldd, whatever his name was, was right. He'd ruined his own life, and destroyed Grace's dreams of happiness with it. He wouldn't play those games, not even to find out what Blackthorn knew of what had happened to Tom. Even if he couldn't find his brother, he wouldn't drag the love of his life down with him. Grace deserved so much more.

He pulled over halfway between Penzance and Penmerryn. He glanced at his phone on the passenger seat, a blue light flashed in the darkness. It was a voice message from Grace. How long had it been there? He played it back, he could hear all too clearly the bitter disappointment in her voice, asking him, yet again, *Where are you?* She had something important to say to him, but it didn't sound like any important news he wanted to hear right now, because he knew, deep down, that Keldd was right. She was finally giving up. And why shouldn't she? Why keep giving him chance after chance. She should have given up on him a long time ago. He knew that, and the kindest thing he could do was to let her go.

A quiet sense of peace washed over him as he put the car into gear and pulled back out onto the road. It was an unfamiliar sensation, he realised. The knowledge that he was at long last making the right decision. He continued driving towards Penmerryn, but instead of making a left at the harbour, he continued along the coast road and up towards the headland. Where he could be alone.

The narrow road climbed higher and higher, threading its way through the rocky landscape. Some would say it was a barren place, windswept and harsh, at the mercy of the elements, but in the darkness of Winter it felt like the only place Daniel could be where he could no longer be plagued by his own thoughts. He swung the car into one of the parking bays, and sat there in the comfort of the dark. Once his eyes adjusted he realised it wasn't truly dark at all. The lights of nearby towns and villages glittered like tiny jewels in the distance, reflecting their upside down worlds in the still water below. Life would go on, people would be happy, they would eat and work, and meet and fall in love, and laugh. Everything a person should do. Including Grace. She should be happy most of all, because god knows she'd not been given much of that so far. It was a good place for her to start again. She had a home, friends, and a job. She would be fine. No, not fine, she would be so much better without him.

Opening the door he stepped out onto the tarmac, momentarily buffeted by the wind he steadied himself. Pulled his coat a little tighter. The coast path lay just below this parking area and he stepped over the grassy curbside and down a small incline until his feet met gravel. A small wooden bench had been carefully placed here to provide the perfect view out across the glorious expanse of blue that would stretch for miles. He could see it against the night sky though, the reverse image of a sunlit daytime world. The photographic negative version it became as night fell. A world of muted greys, and blacks. How had he never noticed there were so many shades of black?

He stepped closer to the edge. An edge he couldn't see, but knew was there. A row of large rocks had been set here, to prevent anyone from accidentally getting too close, but he climbed effortlessly over them to the other side. Silence was so blissful. Euphoric even. Dan wondered how he'd ever coped before with so much chattering in his head, endless words that battered and tormented with their sharp jibes and rough edges.

He didn't want to ever go back to that.

He stepped back instinctively as a sudden clatter of falling stones and dirt dropped away down the cliff, just inches from where he stood. He had reached the edge, as far as he could go. But perhaps not quite. Would it be that easy? To push just that little bit further?

He closed his eyes against the world. Took one step forward and felt the abyss beneath his foot, waiting, like the gaping maw of some giant sea creature of legend. He could almost feel it's hot, fetid, breath rising up to swallow him. He heard a sound, *that whisper*. His head whipped around, eyes searching the black silhouettes around him. That sound wasn't natural. It wasn't meant to be there. It never had!

Then out of the silence it came, something on the wind, like bells. If those twinkling lights of distant towns had a sound, it would be this. Drums came next, a low throb that sent vibrations through the ground, through every bone and sinew in his body. Lights came up over the headland and a great clamouring of sound assaulted his senses. People marching, footsteps moving in unison to a familiar beat, laughter and bells. Oh those bells. Harmonies he'd never imagined, the very essence of light itself. A procession of people clad in white carried lanterns of all shapes and sizes. Lanterns fashioned of paper, woodland berries, and greenery, lit from within by any means. Fairy lights and fire. Then came bare torches, flames that licked and curled and steamed in the cool night air. Flames that ate up the darkness and swallowed it whole.

The procession moved steadily along the path now, its flow not willing to be interrupted by anything. Neither rock nor man. Like a riverbed carved out over centuries the water ebbs and flows, but never forgets its route. Daniel stood by, his eyes wet and glistening as the music flowed through him, and the lights drew him to follow.

"Daniel? Daniel...what are you doing here?" Grace shouted, struggling to be heard above the noise. "Dan?"

He saw her separate from the crowd. A vision in white, her brown winter coat and woolly hat beneath the wispy material. She carried a small lantern on a stick which glowed with a warm yellow light and sparkled in her eyes. She looked so happy to see him. "Grace?" He murmured.

She swept him up, and arms interlocked, they moved as one within the procession. She laughed, said something to him that he couldn't quite catch and he smiled back at her in wonder.

The procession followed the cliff path all the way down into Penmerryn, gathering in the tiny cove amid the fishing boats. The small cafe was open and its staff brought out trays of mulled wine and juice for all. Daniel still felt dazed when the sound of a microphone being tapped stilled the crowd and a hush fell. So quiet all you could hear was the sound of the waves softly washing against the sand.

"Thank you all for coming!" Said the disembodied voice, from a small stage somewhere near the cafe. "This year's Wintertide has been our most successful yet, and it's all because of you... our wonderful supporters and volunteers!" A roar of approval and round of applause rumbled into the night. "Once more we have followed the steps of our ancestors in order to bring light, love and hope back into the world." A tall figure held the microphone, a woman Dan didn't recognise, she wore a costume of white, like the others but as she spoke she stepped aside to welcome another figure. A man dressed in the Devil costume that Dan had seen that day at the Community centre. The Punch and Judy figure dressed in red, with a floppy hat and distorted mask covering his face.

"With our lanterns we come forth this Wintertide to drive out the darkness, to drive out the devils among us, and celebrate the return of the light. We welcome back to us hope for the Spring and Summer to come, may it be prosperous and bring us much happiness for this year ahead! Happy solstice my friends, and we wish you all a merry christmas and a very peaceful new year!"

The crowd roared yet again and Daniel felt the surge of energy and emotion lift him. He looked around and saw the people of his community, some he knew, and some he didn't, but he felt part of something like he never had before.

Grace laughed and cheered, smiling and waving at people he didn't know, and for once he didn't even feel jealous, he just felt ridiculously happy. Like his heart would burst. He swept Grace up in his arms and pulled her to him and held her tightly. She would never know how close he'd come to losing her.

They walked home from the celebrations that went on late into the night. Dan had told her he'd parked up at the headland, and she assumed it was to meet them along the way. It was like they'd stepped back in time. Like the days when they first met and used to meet at the local for a half lager and a G&T. Silly, carefree times. Playing pool, or drunkenly flinging sharp objects at a dartboard. How had things ever gone so wrong?

They fell into bed, longing for sleep, and Daniel longed for this night to never end, because while it seemed like a dream, he didn't really believe it could last. And that come the morning, and the cold light of day, things would be as bad as they ever were, and he'd have to face the fact that he and Grace were not meant to be.

"What's up misery?" She smirked, rolling over to face him.

He stared forlornly at her.

"Hey?" She sat up. "Seriously, what's wrong? We had such a good time yesterday."

"We did. The best! It was like the old days…"

"But better..." She grinned again, "I didn't think you were coming. I mean... I didn't want to force you seeing as you've not been well lately, but when I saw you there, waiting for me..." A broad smile spread across her face and she bent to kiss him. "I was so happy."

"You looked happy, Grace. Beautiful and happy! Happier than I could ever make you, I know that now."

"What do you mean? I was happy because you came... it wouldn't have been the same without you. I'd probably have gone straight home if you hadn't shown up. It was incredible wasn't it? Walking down the coast path with all those lanterns glowing..." She sighed, and relived the moment with a giggle.

"Listen, Grace. I need to talk to you. I know things have been bad, not just since we moved here. And I know I can't expect you to keep on forgiving me, it's not fair on you."

"Dan -"

"- Let me finish. I'm glad we had last night, I guess it was just nice to be caught up in something, it seemed so unreal. I saw you as I'd not seen you in a long time, and that's all my fault, I know it. And I won't stand in your way Grace. I won't stop you moving on. I just want you to know that!"

She sat open mouthed. "I don't understand what this is about. Are you saying we should... split up?"

"No, no I'm not saying that. But I... I thought

you wanted to leave?"

"Why on earth would you think that?"

"Because.. I… I'm just bad for you Grace. I make you so unhappy. I'm just not ok. And it's not fair to expect you to take care of me. I don't want you to waste your life…"

"Wait, just wait there… you think I would be better off without you? Are you kidding me?" She took his face between her palms. "If you think you're getting off that bloody easily you've another thought coming! I am going nowhere, unless it's with you!"

He stared, uncomprehending. "But… I thought."

"You thought wrong matey!"

"But your message… it said you had something important to talk about."

"Yes, we do. And it is *very* important. We need to sell this house."

"Oh."

"We need to sell it and buy something that needs a lot less work and is a lot less time consuming."

Daniel's eyes gave a flicker of confusion and fear.

Grace laughed, "God you're an idiot sometimes. I'm pregnant. We're going to be parents!" She yelled excitedly. "There's only one promise I want from you, aside from selling the house." She said, suddenly serious again.

"Anything!" He stammered.

"No more running off and disappearing on wild goose chases with keys or brothers or anything… it all ends now. Our baby comes first. Above me, above you and most of all above your Brother. He's gone. And unless the police tell us otherwise, he isn't coming back."

"Agreed. 100% agreed. I can't believe it… Grace, I… don't know what to say?"

"Say you're happy. That's all I need."

CHAPTER 17 - A DEBT
MUST ALWAYS BE PAID

It was an unusually warm, sunny day for February. Not known for being the nicest of the winter months, this one seemed different. Not least because the sun was shining, but the sale of Fourlanes house was all going like clockwork. A buyer had been found almost as soon as it had gone on the market, full asking price accepted. And Daniel and Grace had found their new home. A modest two bed cottage on the edge of town, and most importantly, minimal work needed to make it livable for their new family.

Daniel pulled up outside the Estate agents office in the high street. One last bit of paperwork to drop off and fingers crossed, it would all be plain sailing from here. He pushed open the glass door and gave a nod to Jenny, the agent handling the sale. She took the papers and grinned, phone tucked under her chin as she spoke to another client.

Daniel spied his favourite coffee shop two doors down and decided his efforts deserved a large toffee latte as a reward. It was busy, it always was though. He slipped inside, weaving past folks who were leaving with their takeaway coffees, or searching for a seat in the small, cosy cafe. It always smelled so good, nothing could beat the aroma of fresh coffee and baking. He eyed the caramel doughnuts and wondered if Grace would thank him or curse him for bringing one home for her.

Placing his order, he didn't queue for long before the assistant bagged up the doughnuts and handed him the steaming, takeaway cup, but when he held up his debit card she waved it away with a grin. "It's already been paid for Sir."

He looked at her in confusion. "By who?"

The girl nodded hurriedly, wanting to move swiftly on to the next customer, "The gentlemen over there said he owed you a favour, he said something about *always paying his debts*." She shrugged.

Daniel turned his head, it felt like he was moving through treacle. Time seemed to come to a screeching halt as he searched through a sea of faces before he found the one she had motioned to. Silhouetted against the bright sunlight, a man held the door open for a woman with a young toddler, who thanked him, gratefully, and when he glanced up at Daniel, those dark, dead eyes pierced him like a poisoned dart. Mr Blackthorn bowed his head, as though he tipped a hat to Daniel, before scurrying out onto the street like some escaping rodent.

His feet turned to lead and the smell of coffee suddenly made him nauseous. Suddenly aware that he was getting in the way, he apologised, and stepped outside. He looked nervously up and down the street, but of course, there was no sign.

Daniel leaned against the nearest wall to catch his breath. His head was swimming as if he'd just spent the last hour in the pub. Wasn't this all meant to be over? He couldn't face it again. Not now. Not when life was going so well.

Grace was in the garden when he arrived home. She'd wrapped up well, but the unseasonal sunshine had drawn her outside to huddle on the patio chair with a blanket. She looked up at the rustle of a paper bag and pounced on the bakery treat with glee. Daniel was quiet. He sat beside her with the remnants of his cooling coffee in hand.

"Did it all go ok?" Grace asked.

"Mmm…"

"What's up then? Did they mess up your coffee?" She smiled.

"No, it's nothing. How's your doughnut?"

"Bloody fantastic. You not having one? Oh… I nearly forgot, someone left something for you."

"What?" He asked apprehensively.

"I don't know, they just knocked and left it on the doorstep. It's on the table."

He stood and slowly went back inside to the kitchen table, where Grace had left this mysterious parcel. A plain brown package with Daniel's name scrawled in black ink lay there. He thought he might throw up, but he opened it anyway. Inside was a small black box. His hand shook. It felt smooth and shiny to the touch. Just like it had before, but this time it had a stickiness to it, like tar. He pushed it back into the packaging and strode outside to the bin, throwing it inside.

"It's just some rubbish an advertising company keeps sending me. I've told them I'm not interested." He muttered to Grace's questioning look.

"Oh. Fair enough." She shrugged. "Listen, why don't we go out for a walk. Clear the cobwebs. It's too nice to be stuck here, we could go down to the beach."

"Sounds like a plan to me!" He smiled.

They strolled hand in hand down the hill into Penmerryn. The harbour was quiet. A few folk were out walking their dogs, or heading to the pub, but the place was theirs alone. As the winter afternoon drew in, the clear blue sky turned gradually from blue to purple. They continued walking up the headland bathed in sunset colours that picked out the tips of the waves.

Grace sighed happily. "I can't imagine living in London any more."

"You don't wish we could go back then?"
"No way. Do you?" She asked in surprise.
Daniel paused to think. Did he?

"Dan...Seriously?"

"I don't think so. Cornwall is way nicer, but I don't know...maybe one day."

Grace jabbed him in the arm. "Stop thinking about stuff that doesn't matter anymore. It's done and we've moved on."

"I know."

"Oh I meant to tell you, the other day I heard someone talking about that old stone circle we went to. Carn Madrow. It's got quite a story!"

"Oh, really?" Carn Madrow was the last place he wanted to be reminded of right now.

"The local legend goes that a demon lived in an old farmhouse up there on a crossroads, and he would tempt villagers with gifts or treats, and trap them when he got bored of playing his games."

Daniel felt suddenly as if the floor dropped away beneath him. "Who told you that nonsense?" he said. "Sounds like something Ellie would say."

"No, it wasn't Ellie. It was a lovely old lady who works at the library. Anyway, they say the stone circle is known as *the dancing devils*, because the stones are made up of people who made pacts with this devil and never managed to escape. I don't remember seeing a farmhouse up there, do you?"

"Nope." he said.

"Maybe we should go and look for it, could be a bit of fun?"

"Nah. Not interested. Too much hassle just getting up there, besides, there are far more interesting spots on the coastline to investigate. All those beaches and secret coves and tin mine ruins."

"Hmm well, I suppose so. I just thought you'd be interested. I do prefer being by the sea, it feels so free up here." She took in a deep breath of sea air and threw out her arms. "Blissss!" She sighed. "But speaking of Ellie…"

Daniel grimaced.

"I did hear back from her. She spent Christmas with family *up country*, and she's glad things have worked out for us. To tell you the truth I'm not sure she wants to come back. She mentioned she'd been offered a job up there, so…"

Dan shrugged. "A change might be good for her."

"That's what I said."

"It's funny how that happens isn't it?" Daniel looked thoughtful. "One minute you think your life is all mapped out, and then you blink and it's all different."

Grace didn't need to reply. They both knew only too well the fragility of life.

That night, as Daniel closed the bedroom curtains he stole a glance down at the magnolia tree. Its branches were in full bud now, preparing to burst forth in all their brilliance. How happy Grace had been to see it when they'd moved in, and how excited she had been to see her first Cornish spring. Well with any luck their first spring would be far away from this house, and that tree. That tree where it had all begun did not feel like a good omen and he hoped never to see those blooms fall.

He slept deeply. His dreams had been quiet for months now. But tonight, something squirmed within his mind. Uninvited, an inky blackness swam like a sickness, through the borders of this dreamworld.

Daniel stood now at the crossroads, in full view of the farmhouse. Only it was no longer a ruin. In his dream it looked newly built. The walls, intact. The white paint on the window frames and front door, neat and pristine. He walked towards the house as smoke billowed from its narrow chimney. Somebody was home.

A sudden crack like lightning seemed to come from behind and the sound spun him on his heels. A man appeared out of thin air. Strong, sturdy, average build. He wore old fashioned clothing, rough tweed, a white shirt, and a hat. He strode forward, head tilted downwards.

As he passed Daniel he nodded, tipped his hat. Something in that gesture made Dan feel uneasy. The man stepped across the threshold and removed his hat. He held in one hand a small black box and as he turned, Daniel realised that he recognised Mr Blackthorn for just an instant, in that same beady eyed animal stare. And just before the door slammed shut he also saw, in the room behind Mr Blackthorn, stood two men. They were held fast by seemingly invisible chains, and their mouths screamed in silent howls.

He recognised those men too. For they were his family.

THE END

About The Author

Julia Guthrie was born in Cambridgeshire in 1974, and currently lives with her Husband in Lincolnshire, after having spent almost 20 years in Cornwall.
During this time she had a successful art career, but in recent years she has put down her paintbrushes and turned her hand to writing both fantasy, and
horror short stories and novels.
Julia is a huge fan of the folk horror genre, and is also an avid player of RPG games such as Witcher and Skyrim.

Email:juliaguthrieauthor@outlook.com
Facebook:www.facebook.com/juliaguthrieauthor

Printed in Dunstable, United Kingdom